Jeff De Booy

Carol Sheilds was born in Oak Park, Illinois, and has made Canada her home since 1957. She studied at Hanover College and the University of Ottawa. A prolific writer, her books include *Others, Intersect, Small Ceremonies, The Box Garden, Happenstance, A Fairly Conventional Woman, Various Miracles,* and *Swann: A Mystery.* She lives and writes in Winnipeg.

THE ORANGE FISH

Carol Shields

VINTAGE CONTEMPORARIES

VINTAGE BOOKS • A DIVISION OF RANDOM HOUSE • TORONTO

FIRST VINTAGE BOOKS EDITION, MARCH 1990

Copyright © 1989 by Carol Shields

All rights reserved under International and Pan-American
Copyright Conventions.

Originally published in Canada in 1989 by Random House of
Canada Limited Toronto.

Canadian Cataloguing in Publication Data

Shields, Carol, 1935-
The orange fish

ISBN 0-394-22118-4

I. Title.

PS8587.H46073 1989   C813'.54   C89-093810-5
PR9199.3.S55073 1989

Cover design: Brant Cowie/ArtPlus Limited
Cover painting: *Skater* (1988) by Jane Zednik

The following stories have been published previously: "The
Orange Fish" in *A Room of One's Own*; "Chemistry" in *The
Canadian Forum*; "Today Is the Day" in *The WEst Coast
REview* under the title "Close Observation"; "Good Manners"
in *The WEst Coast REview*; "Times of Sickness and Health" in
A Room of One's Own; "Family Secrets" in *Prism
International*; "Fuel for the Fire" in *Border Crossings*; "Milk
Bread Beer Ice" in *Saturday Night*; "Hinterland" and "Block
Out" in *Prairie Fire*.

Printed and bound in Canada

For

Joan and Shad

and Mary Lou

CONTENTS

The Orange Fish

Like others of my generation I am devoted to food, money, and sex; but I have an ulcer and have been unhappily married to Lois-Ann, a lawyer, for twelve years. As you might guess, we are both fearful of aging. Recently Lois-Ann showed me an article she had clipped from the newspaper, a profile of a well-known television actress who was described as being "deep in her thirties."

"That's what we are," Lois-Ann said sadly, "deep in our thirties." She looked at me from behind a lens of tears.

Despite our incompatibility, the two of us understand each other, and I knew more or less what it was she was thinking: that some years ago, when she was twenty-five, she made up her mind to go to Vancouver Island and raise dahlias, but on the very day she bought her air ticket, she got a letter in the mail saying she'd been accepted at law school. "None of us writes our own script," she said to me once, and of course she's right. I still toy–I confess this to you freely–with my old fantasy of running a dude ranch, with the thought of well-rubbed saddles and harnesses and the whole sweet leathery tip of possibility, even though I know the dude market's been depressed for a decade, dead in fact.

Not long ago, on a Saturday morning, Lois-Ann and I had one of our long talks about values, about goals. The mood as we sat over breakfast was sternly analytical.

"Maybe we've become trapped in the cult of consumerism and youth worship," I suggested.

"Trapped by our *zeitgeist*," said Lois-Ann, who has a way of capping a point, especially my point.

A long silence followed, twenty seconds, thirty seconds. I glanced up from an emptied coffee cup, remembered that my fortieth birthday was only weeks away, and felt a flare of panic in my upper colon. The pain was hideous and familiar. I took a deep breath as I'd been told to do. Breathe in, then out. Repeat. The trick is to visualize the pain, its substance and color, and then transfer it to a point outside the body. I concentrated on a small spot above our breakfast table, a random patch on the white wall. Often this does the trick, but this morning the blank space, the smooth drywall expanse of it, seemed distinctly accusing.

At one time Lois-Ann and I had talked about wall-papering the kitchen or at least putting up an electric clock shaped like a sunflower. We also considered a ceramic bas-relief of cauliflowers and carrots, and after that a little heart-shaped mirror bordered with rattan, and, more recently, a primitive map of the world with a practical acrylic surface. We have never been able to agree, never been able to arrive at a decision.

I felt Lois-Ann watching me, her eyes as neat and neutral as birds' eggs. "What we need," I said, gesturing at the void, "is a picture."

"Or possibly a print," said Lois-Ann, and immediately went to get her coat.

Three hours later we were the owners of a cheerful lithograph titled *The Orange Fish*. It was unframed, but enclosed in a sandwich of twinkling glass, its corners secured by a set of neat metal clips. The mat surrounding the picture was a generous three inches in width–we liked that–and the background was a shimmer of green; within this space the orange fish was suspended.

I wish somehow you might see this fish. He is boldly drawn, and just as boldly colored. He occupies approximately eighty per cent of the surface and has about him a wet, dense look of health. To me, at least, he appears to have stopped moving, to be resting against the wall of green water. A stream of bubbles, each one separate and tear-shaped, floats above him, binding him to his element. Of course he is seen in side profile, as fish always are, and this classic posture underlines the tranquillity of the whole. He possesses, too, a Buddha-like sense of being in the *right* place, the only place. His center, that is, where you might imagine his heart to be, is sweetly orange in color, and this color diminishes slightly as it flows toward the semi-transparency of fins and the round, ridged, non-appraising mouth. But it was his eye I most appreciated, the kind of wide, ungreedy eye I would like to be able to turn onto the world. We made up our minds quickly; he would fit nicely over the breakfast table. Lois-Ann mentioned that the orange tones would pick up the colors of the seat covers. We were in a state of rare agreement. And the price was right.

Forgive me if I seem condescending, but you should know that, strictly speaking, a lithograph is not an original work of art, but rather a print from an original plate; the number of prints is limited to ten or twenty or fifty or more, and this number is always indicated on the piece itself. A tiny inked set of numbers in the corner, just beneath the artist's signature, will tell you, for example, that our particular fish is number eight out of an existing ten copies, and I think it pleased me from the start to think of those other copies, the nine brother fish scattered elsewhere, suspended in identical seas of green water, each pointed soberly in the same leftward direction. I found myself in a fanciful mood, humming, installing a hook on the kitchen wall, and hanging our new acquisition. We stepped backward to admire it, and later Lois-Ann made a Spanish omelet with fresh fennel, which we ate beneath the austere eye of our beautiful fish.

As you well know, there are certain necessary tasks that coarsen the quality of everyday life, and while Lois-Ann and I went about ours, we felt calmed by the heft of our solemn, gleaming fish. My health improved from the first day, and before long Lois-Ann and I were on better terms, often sharing workaday anecdotes or pointing out curious items to each other in the newspaper. I rediscovered the girlish angularity of her arms and shoulders as she wriggled in and out of her little nylon nightgowns, smoothing down the skirts with a sly, sweet glance in my direction. For the first time in years she left the lamp burning on the bedside table and, as in our early days, she covered me with kisses, a long nibbling trail up and down the ridge of my vertebrae. In the morning, drinking our coffee at the breakfast table, we looked up, regarded our orange fish, smiled at each other, but were ritualistically careful to say nothing.

We didn't ask ourselves, for instance, what kind of fish this was, whether it was a carp or a flounder or a monstrously out-of-scale goldfish. Its biological classification, its authenticity, seemed splendidly irrelevant. Details, just details; we swept them aside. What mattered was the prismatic disjection of green light that surrounded it. What mattered was that it existed. That it had no age, no history. It simply *was.* You can understand that to speculate, to analyze overmuch, interferes with that narrow gap between symbol and reality, and it was precisely in the folds of that little gap that Lois-Ann and I found our temporary refuge.

Soon an envelope arrived in the mail, an official notice. We were advised that the ten owners of *The Orange Fish* met on the third Thursday evening of each month. The announcement was photocopied, but on decent paper with an appropriate logo. Eight-thirty was the regular time, and there was a good-natured reminder at the bottom of the page about the importance of getting things going punctually.

Nevertheless we were late. At the last minute Lois-Ann discovered a run in her pantyhose and had to change. I had difficulty getting the car started, and of course traffic was heavy. Furthermore, the meeting was in a part of the city that was unfamiliar to us. Lois-Ann, although a clever lawyer, has a poor sense of spatial orientation and told me to turn left when I should have turned right. And then there was the usual problem with parking, for which she seemed to hold me responsible. We arrived at eight-forty-five, rather agitated and out of breath from climbing the stairs.

Seeing that roomful of faces, I at first experienced a shriek in the region of my upper colon. Lois-Ann had a similar shock of alarm, what she afterwards described to me as a jolt to her imagination, as though an axle in her left brain had suddenly seized.

Someone was speaking as we entered the room. I recognized the monotone of the born chairman. "It is always a pleasure," the voice intoned, "to come together, to express our concerns and compare experiences."

At that moment the only experience I cared about was the sinuous river of kisses down my shoulders and backbone, but I managed to sit straight on my folding chair and to look alert and responsible. Lois-Ann, in lawyerlike fashion, inspected the agenda, running a little gold pencil down the list of items, her tongue tight between her teeth.

The voice rumbled on. Minutes from the previous meeting were read and approved. There was no old business. Nor any new business. "Well, then," the chairman said, "who would like to speak first?"

Someone at the front of the room rose and gave his name, a name that conveyed the double-pillared boom of money and power. I craned my neck, but could see only a bush of fine white hair. The voice was feeble yet dignified, a persisting quaver from a soft old silvery throat, and I realized after a minute or two that we were listening to a testimonial. A mystical experience was described. Something, too, about the "search for definitions" and about "wandering in the wilderness" and about the historic symbol of the fish in the Western Tradition, a secret sign, an icon expressing providence. "My life has been altered," the voice concluded, "and given direction."

The next speaker was young, not more than twenty I would say. Lois-Ann and I took in the flare of dyed hair, curiously angled and distinctively punk in style. You can imagine our surprise: here of all places to find a spiked bracelet, black nails, cheeks outlined in blue paint, and a forehead tattooed with the world's most familiar expletive. *The Orange Fish* had been a graduation gift from his parents. The framing alone cost two hundred dollars. He had stared at it for weeks, or possibly months, trying to understand what it meant; then revelation rushed in. "Fishness" was a viable alternative. The orange fins and sneering mouth said no to "all that garbage that gets shoveled on your head by society. So keep swimming and don't take any junk," he wound up, then sat down to loud applause.

A woman in a neatly tailored mauve suit spoke for a quarter of an hour about her investment difficulties. She'd tried stocks. She'd tried the bond market. She'd tried treasury bills and mutual funds. In every instance she found herself buying at the peak and selling just as the market bottomed out. Until she found out about investing in art. Until she found *The*

Orange Fish. She was sure, now, that she was on an upward curve. That success was just ahead. Recently she had started to be happy, she said.

A man rose to his feet. He was in his mid-fifties, we guessed, with good teeth and an aura of culture lightly worn. "Let me begin at the beginning," he said. He had been through a period of professional burn-out, arriving every day at his office exhausted. "Try to find some way to brighten up the place," he told his secretary, handing her a blank check. *The Orange Fish* appeared the next day. Its effect had been instantaneous: on himself, his staff, and also on his clients. It was as though a bright banner had been raised. Orange, after all, was the color of celebration, and it is the act of celebration which has been crowded out of contemporary life.

The next speaker was cheered the moment he stood. He had, we discovered, traveled all the way from Japan, from the city of Kobe–making our little journey across the city seem trivial. As you can imagine, his accent was somewhat harsh and halting, but I believe we understood something of what he said. In the small house where he lives, he has hung *The Orange Fish* in the traditional tokonoma alcove, just above the black lacquered slab of wood on which rests a bowl of white flowers. The contrast between the sharp orange of the fish's scales and the unearthly whiteness of the flowers' petals reminds him daily of the contradictions that abound in the industrialized world. At this no one clapped louder than myself.

A fish is devoid of irony, someone else contributed in a brisk, cozy voice, and is therefore a reminder of our lost innocence, of the era which predated double meanings and trial balloons. But, at the same time, a fish is more and also less than its bodily weight.

A slim, dark-haired woman, hardly more than a girl, spoke for several minutes about the universality of fish. How three-quarters of the earth's surface is covered with water, and in this water leap fish by the millions. There are people in this world, she said, who have never seen a sheep or a cow, but there is no one who is not acquainted with the organic shape of the fish.

"We begin our life in water," came a hoarse and boozey squawk from the back row, "and we yearn all our days to return to our natural element. In water we are free to move without effort, to be most truly ourselves."

"The interior life of the fish is unknowable," said the next speaker, who was Lois-Ann. "She swims continuously, and is as mute, as voiceless as a dahlia. She speaks at the level of gesture, in circling patterns revived and repeated. The purpose of her eye is to decode and rearrange the wordless world."

"The orange fish," said a voice which turned out to be my own, "will never grow old."

I sat down. Later my hand was most warmly shaken. During the refreshment hour I was greeted with feeling and asked to sign the membership book. Lois-Ann put her arms around me, publicly, her face shining, and I knew that when we got home she would offer me a cup of cocoa. She would leave the bedside lamp burning and bejewel me with a stream of kisses. You can understand my feeling. Enchantment. Ecstasy. But waking up in the morning we would not be the same people.

I believe we all felt it, standing in that brightly lit

room with our coffee cups and cookies: the woman in the tailored mauve suit, the fiftyish man with the good teeth, even the young boy with his crown of purple hair. We were, each of us, speeding along a trajectory, away from each other, and away from that one fixed point in time, the orange fish.

But how helplessly distorted our perspective turned out to be. What none of us could have known that night was that *we* were the ones who were left behind, sheltered and reprieved by a rare congeniality and by the pleasure that each of us feels when our deepest concerns have been given form.

That very evening, in another part of the city, ten thousand posters of the orange fish were rolling off a press. These posters–which would sell first for $10, then $8.49, and later $1.95–would decorate the rumpled bedrooms of teenagers and the public washrooms of filling stations and beer halls. Within a year a postage stamp would be issued, engraved with the image of the orange fish, but a fish whose eye, miniaturized, would hold a look of mild bewilderment. And sooner than any of us would believe possible, the orange fish would be slapped across the front of a Sears flyer, given a set of demeaning eyebrows, and cruelly bisected with an invitation to stock up early on back-to-school supplies.

There can be no turning back at this point, as you surely know. Winking off lapel buttons and earrings, stamped onto sweatshirts and neckties, doodled on notepads and in the margin of love letters, the orange fish, without a backward glance, will begin to die.

Chemistry

If you were to write me a letter out of the blue, typewritten, handwritten, whatever, and remind me that you were once in the same advanced recorder class with me at the YMCA on the south side of Montreal and that you were the girl given to head colds and black knitted tights and whose *Sprightly Music for the Recorder* had shed its binding, then I would, feigning a little diffidence, try to shore up a coarsened image of the winter of 1972. Or was it 1973? Unforgivable to forget, but at a certain distance the memory buckles; those are the words I'd use.

But you will remind me of the stifling pink heat of the room. The cusped radiators under the windows. How Madam Bessant was always there early, dipping her shoulders in a kind of greeting, arranging sheets of music and making those little throat-clearing

11

chirps of hers, getting things organized–for us, everything for us, for no one else.

The light that leaked out of those winter evenings filled the skirted laps of Lonnie Henry and Cecile Landreau, and you of course, as well as the hollows of your bent elbows and the seam of your upper lip brought down so intently on the little wooden mouthpiece and the bony intimacy of your instep circling in air. You kept time with that circling foot of yours, and also with the measured delay and snap of your chin. We sat in a circle–you will prod me into this remembrance. Our chairs drawn tight together. Those clumsy old-fashioned wooden folding chairs? Dusty slats pinned loosely with metal dowels? A cubist arrangement of stern angles and purposeful curves. Geometry and flesh. Eight of us, counting Madam Bessant.

At seven-thirty sharp we begin, mugs of coffee set to one side. The routines of those weekly lessons are so powerfully set after a few weeks that only the most exigent of emergencies can breach them. We play as one person, your flutey B minor is mine, my slim tonal accomplishment yours. Madam Bessant's blunt womanly elbows rise out sideways like a pair of duck wings and signal for attention. Her fretfulness gives way to authority. *Alors*, she announces, and we begin. Alpine reaches are what we try for. God marching in his ziggurat heaven. Oxygen mists that shiver the scalp. Music so cool and muffled it seems smoothed into place by a thumb. Between pieces we kid around, noodle for clarity, for what Madam Bessant calls roundness of tone, *rondure, rondure.* Music and hunger, accident and intention meet here as truly as they did in the ancient courts of Asia

Minor. *"Pas mal,"* nods our dear Madam, taking in breath, not wanting to handicap us with praise; this a world we're making, after all, not just a jumble of noise. We don't know what to do with all the amorous steam in the room. We're frightened of it, but committed to making more. We start off each lesson with our elementary Mozart bits and pieces from the early weeks, then the more lugubrious Haydn, then Bach, all texture and caution–our small repertoire slowly expanding–and always we end the evening with an intricate new exercise, something tricky to bridge the week, so many flagged, stepped notes crowded together that the page in front of us is black. We hesitate. Falter. Apologize by means of our nervy young laughter. "It will come," encourages Madam Bessant with the unlicensed patience of her métier. We read her true meaning: the pledge that in seven days we'll be back here again, reassembled, another Wednesday night arrived at, our unbroken circle. Foul-mouthed Lonnie H. with her starved-looking fingers ascends a steep scale, and you respond, solidly, distinctively, your head arcing back and forth, back and forth, a neat two-inch slice. The contraction of your throat forms a lovely knot of deliberation. (I loved you more than the others, but, like a monk, allowed myself no distinctions.) On and on, the timid fingerings repeat and repeat, picking up the tempo or slowing it down, putting a sonorous umbrella over our heads, itself made of rain, a translucent roof, temporary, provisional–we never thought otherwise, we never thought at all. Madam Bessant regards her watch. How quickly the time. . . .

In Montreal, in January, on a Wednesday evening. The linoleum-floored basement room is our salon, our conservatory. This is a space carved out of the nutty wood of foreverness. Windows, door, music stands and chairs, all of them battered, all of them worn slick and giving up a craved-for weight of classicism. The walls exude a secretive decaying scent, of human skin, of footwear, of dirty pink paint flaking from the pipes. Half the overhead lights are burned out, but it would shame us to complain. To notice. Madam Bessant–who tolerates the creaky chairs, the grudging spotted ceiling globes, our sprawling bodies, our patched jeans, our cigarette smoke, our outdoor boots leaking slush all over the floor, our long uncombed hair–insists that the door be kept shut during class, this despite the closeness of the overheated air, choking on its own interior odors of jointed ductwork and mice and dirt.

Her baton is a slim metal rod, like a knitting needle–perhaps it *is* a knitting needle–and with this she energetically beats and stirs and prods. At the start of the lessons there seems such an amplitude of time that we can afford to be careless, to chat away between pieces and make jokes about our blunders, always our own blunders, no one else's; our charity is perfect. The room, which by now seems a compaction of the whole gray, silent frozen city, fills up with the reticulation of musical notes, curved lines, spontaneous response, actions, and drawn breath. You have one of your head colds, and between pieces stop and shake cough drops, musically, out of a little blue tin.

Something else happens. It affects us all, even Mr. Mooney with his criminal lips and eyes, even Lonnie

H. who boils and struts with dangerous female smells. We don't just play the music, we *find* it. What opens before us on our music stands, what we carry in with us on our snow-sodden parkas and fuzzed-up hair, we know for the first time, hearing the notes just as they came, unclothed out of another century when they were nothing but small ink splashes, as tentative and quick on their trim black shelves as the finger Madam Bessant raises to her lips–her signal that we are to begin again, at the beginning, again and again.

She is about forty. Old, in our eyes. Not a beauty, not at all, except when she smiles, which is hardly ever. Her face is a somatic oval with a look of having been handled, molded; a high oily worried forehead, but unlined. A pair of eye glasses, plastic framed, and an ardor for clear appraisal that tells you she wore those same glasses, or similar ones, through a long comfortless girlhood, through a muzzy, joyless adolescence, forever breathing on their lenses and attempting to polish them beyond their optical powers, rubbing them on the hems of dragging skirts or the tails of unbecoming blouses. She has short, straight hair, almost black, and wears silvery ear clips, always the same pair, little curly snails of blackened silver, and loose cheap sweaters that sit rawly at the neck. Her neck, surprisingly, is a stem of sumptuous flesh, pink with health, as are her wrists and the backs of her busy, rhythmically rotating hands. On one wrist is a man's gold watch that she checks every few minutes, for she must be home by ten o'clock, as she frequently reminds us, to relieve the baby sitter, a mere girl of fourteen. There are three children at home, all boys–that much we know. Her husband, *a* husband, is not in the picture. Not mentioned, not ever. We sense domestic peril, or even tragedy, the kind of tragedy that bears down without mercy.

Divorce, you think. (This is after class, across the street, drinking beer at Le Piston.) Or widowed. Too young to be a widow, Lonnie H. categorically says. Deserted maybe. Who says that? One of us–Rhonda? Deserted for a younger, more beautiful woman? This seems possible and fulfills an image of drama and pain we are prepared to embrace; we begin to believe it; soon we believe it unconditionally.

We never talk politics after class, not in this privileged love-drugged circle–we've had enough of politics, more than enough. Our talk is first about Madam Bessant, our tender concern for her circumstances, her children, her baby sitter just fourteen years old, her absent husband, her fretful attention to the hour, her sense of having always to hurry away, her coat not quite buttoned or her gloves pulled on. We also discuss endlessly, without a touch of darkness, the various ways each of us has found to circumvent our powerlessness. How to get cheap concert tickets, for instance. How to get on the pogey. Ways to ride the Métro free. How to break a lease, how to badger a landlady into repairing the water heater. Where to go for half-priced baked goods. Cecile Landreau is the one who tells us the name of the baked goods outlet. She has a large, clean ice-maiden face and comes from a little town out west, in Alberta, a town with a rollicking comical name. She gets a laugh every time she mentions it, and she mentions it often. A lively and obstinate girl– you remember–and highly adaptive. She moved to

Montreal just one year before and already she knows where to get things cheap: discount shoes, winter coats direct from the manufacturer, art supplies marked down. She never pays full price. ("You think I'm nuts?") Her alto recorder, a soft pine-colored Yamaha, she bought in a pawn shop for ten dollars and keeps it in a pocketed leather case that she made herself in a leathercraft course, also offered at the Y.

The poverty we insinuate is part real and part desire. We see ourselves as accidental survivors crowded to the shores of a cynical economy. By evasion, by mockery, by a mutual nibbling away at substance, we manage to achieve a dry state of asceticism that feeds on itself. We live on air and water or nothing at all; you would think from the misty way we talk we had never heard of parents or cars or real estate or marital entanglements. The jobs we allude to are seasonal and casual, faintly amusing, mildly degrading. So are our living arrangements and our live-in companions. For the sake of each other, out of our own brimming imaginations, we impoverish ourselves, but this is not a burdensome poverty; we exalt in it, and with our empty pockets and eager charity, we're prepared to settle down after our recorder lesson at a corner table in Le Piston and nurse a single beer until midnight.

But Mr. Mooney is something else. Hungry for membership in our ranks, he insists loudly on buying everyone a second round, and a third. Robert is his first name, Robert Mooney. He speaks illiterate French and appalling English. Reaching into his back pocket for his wallet, a thick hand gripping thick leather, he's cramped by shadows, blurred of feature, older than the rest of us, older by far, maybe even in his fifties, one of those small, compact, sweet-eyed, supple-voiced men you used to see floating around certain quarters of Montreal, ducking behind tabloids or grabbing short ryes or making endless quick phone calls from public booths.

Here in Le Piston, after our recorder lesson, he drops a handful of coins on the table and some bills, each one a transparent, childish offer of himself. My round, he says, without a shred of logic. He has stubby blackened fingers and alien appetites, also built-up shoes to give himself height, brutal hair oil, gold slashes in his back teeth. We drink his beer down fast, without pleasure, ashamed. He watches us, beaming.

All he wants is a portion of our love, and this we refuse. Our reasons are discreditable. His generosity. His age. His burnished leather coat, the way it fits snugly across his round rump. His hair oil and puttied jowls. Stubble, pores, a short thick neck, history. The way the beer foam nudges up against his dark lip. Any minute he's likely to roister or weep or tell a joke about a Jew and a Chinaman or order a plate of *frites*. The joke, if he tells it, we'll absorb without blinking; the *frites* we'll consume down to the last crystal of salt. Dispassionate acts performed out of our need to absolve him. To absolve ourselves.

Robert Mooney is a spoiler, a pernicious interloper who doesn't even show up until the third Wednesday when we've already done two short Mozart pieces and are starting in on Haydn, but there he is in the doorway, his arms crossed over his boxer's chest. A shuffling awkward silence, then mumbled introductions, and bad grace all around except for Madam Bessant who doesn't even notice. Doesn't even *notice*. Our seven stretches to eight. An extra chair is found, clatteringly unfolded and squashed between yours and Pierre's. (Pierre of the cowboy boots and gold earring, as though you need reminding.) Into this chair Mr. Mooney collapses, huffing hard and scrambling with his thick fingers to find his place in the book Madam Bessant kindly lends him until he has an opportunity to buy one of his own.

Layers of incongruity radiate around him: the unsecured history that begs redemption, rough questions stored in silence. How has this man, for instance, this Robert Mooney, acquired a taste for medieval instruments in the first place? And by what manner has he risen to the advanced level? And through what mathematical improbability has he come into contact with Mozart and with the gentle Madam Bessant and the YMCA Winter Enrichment Program and with us, our glare of nonrecognition? When he chomps on his mouthpiece with his moist monkey mouth we think of cigars or worse. With dwindling inattention he caresses his instrument, which is old and beautifully formed. He fingers the openings clumsily, yet is able to march straight through the first exercise with a rhythm so vigorous and unhesitating you'd think he'd been preparing it for months. He has nothing of your delicacy, of course, nor Pierre's even, and he can't begin to sight read the way Rhonda can–remember Rhonda? Of course you remember Rhonda, who could forget her? Mr. Mooney rides roughshod over poor Rhonda, scrambles right past her with his loud marching notes blown sharply forward as if he were playing a solo. *"Bon,"* Madam Bessant says to him after he bursts through to the end of his second lesson. She addresses him in exactly the same tone she uses for us, employing the same little fruited nodes of attention. "Clearly you know how to phrase," she tells him, and her face cracks with a rare smile.

The corners of our mouths tuck in; withholding, despising. But what is intolerable in our eyes is our own intolerance, so shabby and sour beside Madam Bessant's spontaneously bestowed praise. We can't bear it another minute; we surrender in a cloudburst of sentiment. And so, by a feat of inversion, Robert Mooney wins our love and enters our circle, enters it raggedly but forever. His contradictions, his ruptured history, match our own–if the truth were known. Seated at the damp table at Le Piston he opens his wallet yet again and buys rounds of beer, and at the end of the evening, on a slicked white street, with the moon shrunk down to a chip, we embrace him.

We embrace each other, all of us, a rough huddle of wool outerwear and arms, our cold faces brushing together, our swiftly applied poultice of human flesh.

It was Rhonda of all people, timorous Rhonda, who initiated the ceremonial embrace after our first lesson and trip to Le Piston. Right there on the sidewalk, acting out of who knows what wild impulse, she simply threw open her arms and invited us in. We were shy the first time, not used to being so suddenly enfolded, not knowing where it would lead. We were also young and surprised to be let loose in the world so soon, trailing with us our differently colored branches of experience, terrified at presuming or pushing up too close. If it had been anyone other than Rhonda offering herself, we might have held back, but who could refuse her outspread arms and the particularity of her smooth camel coat? (Do you agree? Tell me yes or no.) The gravest possible pleasure was offered and seized, this hugging, this not-quite kiss.

Already after three weeks it's a rite, our end-of-evening embrace, rather solemn but with a suggestion of benediction, each of us taken in turn by the others and held for an instant, a moonlit choreographed spectacle. At this moment our ardor grows dangerous and threatens to overflow. This extemporaneous kind of street-love paralyzes the unsteady. (The youth of the eighties would snort to see it.) One step further and we'd be actors in a shabby old play, too loaded with passion to allow revision. For that reason we keep our embrace short and chaste, but the whole evening, the whole week in fact, bends toward this dark public commerce of arms and bodies and the freezing murmur that accompanies it. Until next week. Next Wednesday. (A passport, a guarantee of safe conduct.) *A la prochaine.*

One night in early March Rhonda appears in class with red eyes. The redness matches the long weepy birthmark that starts beneath her left ear and spills like rubbery fluid down the side of her neck.

You glance up at her and notice, then open your big woven bag for a Kleenex. "It's the wind," you say, to spare her. "There's nothing worse than a March wind." We're well into Bach by this time and, of all of us, Rhonda handles Bach with the greatest ease. This you remember, how she played with the unsupported facility that comes from years of private lessons, not that she ever mentions this, not a word of it, and not that we inquire. We've learned, even Mr. Mooney has learned, to fall back and allow Rhonda to lead us through the more difficult passages. But tonight her energy is frighteningly reduced. She falters and slides and, finally, halfway through the new piece, puts down her recorder, just places it quietly on the floor beneath her chair and runs, hobbling unevenly, out of the room.

Madam Bessant is bewildered–her eyes open wide behind her specs–but she directs us to carry on, and we do, limping along to an undistinguished conclusion. Then Lonnie H. goes off in search of Rhonda.

Lonnie H. is a riddle, a paradox. Her hair is as densely, dully orange as the plastic shopping bag in which she carries her portfolio of music and the beaded leather flip-flops she wears during class. That walk of hers–she walks with the savage assurance of the young and combative, but on Wednesday night at least she tries to keep her working-class spite in check; you can see her sucking in her breath and biting down on those orange lips.

Later, when we're doing our final exercise, the two of them, Rhonda and Lonnie H., reappear. A consultation has been held in the corridor or in the washroom. Rhonda is smiling fixedly. Lonnie H. is looking wise and sad. "An affair of the heart," she whispers to us later as we put on our coats and prepare to cross the street to Le Piston. An affair of the heart–the phrase enters my body like an injection of sucrose, its improbable sweetness. It's not what we've come to expect of the riddlesome Lonnie. But she says it knowingly–an affair of the heart–and the words soften her tarty tangle-haired look of anarchy, make her almost serene.

Some time later, weeks later or perhaps that very night, I see Pierre with his warpish charm reach under the table at Le Piston and take Rhonda's hand in his. He strokes her fingers as though he possesses the fire of invention. He has a set of neglected teeth, a stammer, and there is something amiss with his scalp, a large roundness resembling, under the strands of his lank Jesus hair, a wreath of pink plastic. His chin is short and witty, his long elastic body ambiguous. The left ear, from which a gold hoop dangles, is permanently inflamed.

It is Pierre who tells us one evening the truth about Madam Bessant's husband. The story has reached him through a private and intricately convoluted family pipeline: the ex-husband of a cousin of Pierre's sister-in-law (or something of this order) once lived in the same apartment block as Monsieur and Madam Bessant, on the same floor in fact, and remembered that the nights were often disturbed by the noise of crying babies and the sound of Monsieur Bessant, who was a piano teacher, playing Chopin, often the same nocturne again and again, always the same. When the piano playing stopped abruptly one day, the neighbors assumed that someone had complained. There was also a rumor, because he was no longer seen coming or going, that Monsieur Bessant was sick. This rumor was verified one morning, suddenly and terribly, by the news of his death. He had, it seemed, collapsed in a downtown Métro station on a steamy summer day, just toppled off the platform into the path of an approaching train. And one more detail. Pierre swallows as he says it. The head was completely separated from the body.

What are we to do with this story? We sit for some time in silence. It is a story too filled with lesions and hearsay, yet it is also, coming from the artless, stammering Pierre, curiously intact. All its elements fit; its sequence is wholly convincing–Monsieur Bessant, swaying dizzily one minute and cut to ribbons the next, people screaming, the body collected and identified, the family informed, heat rising in waves and deforming the future. Everything altered, changed forever.

"Of course it might have been a heart attack," Pierre says, wanting now to cancel the whole account and go back to the other, simpler story of an unfeeling husband who abandons his wife for a younger woman.

"Or a stroke," Cecile Landreau suggests. "A stroke is not all that unusual, even for a quite young man. I could tell you stories."

Robert Mooney keeps his eyes on the chilly neck of his beer bottle. And he keeps his mouth clapped shut. All the while the rest of us offer theories for Monsieur Bessant's sudden collapse–heat stroke, low blood sugar–Robert keeps a hard silence. "A helluva shock" is all he says, and then mumbles, "for her."

A stranger entering Le Piston and overhearing us might think we were engaged in careless gossip. And, seeing Pierre reach for Rhonda's hand under the table, might suspect carnal pressure. Or infer something flirtatious about Cecile Landreau, toying with her charm bracelet in a way that solicits our protection. And calculating greed (or worse, condescension) in our blithe acceptance of Robert Mooney's rounds of beer. Lonnie H. in a knitted muffler, pungent with her own bodily scent, could easily be misunderstood and her cynical, slanging raptures misread. A stranger could never guess at the kind of necessity, innocent of the sensual, the manipulative, that binds us together, that has begun as early as that first lesson when we entered the room and saw Madam Bessant tensely handing out purple mimeographed sheets and offsetting the chaos of our arrival. We were ashamed in those first few minutes, ashamed to have come. We felt compromised, awkward, wanting badly to explain ourselves, why we were there. We came to learn, we might have said had anyone asked, to advance, to go forward, something of that order. Nothing crystallizes good impulses so much as the wish to improve one's self. This is one of the things that doesn't change.

After that first night, we relaxed. The tang of the schoolroom played to our affections and so did the heat of our closely drawn chairs, knees almost touching so that the folds of your skirt aligned with my thigh, though from all appearances you failed to notice. The fretfulness with which Madam Bessant regarded her watch put us on our honor, declared meanness and mischief out of bounds, demanded that we make the allotted time count–and so we brought our best selves and nothing else. Our youth, our awkwardness, our musical naiveté yoked good will to virtue, as sacredness attaches itself invisibly to certain rare moments.

I exaggerate, I romanticize–I can hear you say this, your smiling reproach. I have already, you claim, given poor Pierre an earring and a stammer, accorded Lonnie H. an orange plastic bag and a sluttish mouth, branded Rhonda with the humiliation of a port-wine birthmark when a small white scar was all she had or perhaps only its psychic equivalent, high up on her cheek, brushed now and then unconsciously with the back of her hand. But there's too much density in the basement room to stop for details.

Especially now with our time so short, five more weeks, four more weeks. Some nights we linger at Le Piston until well after midnight, often missing the last train home, preferring to walk rather than cut our time short. Three more weeks. Our final class is the fourteenth of May and we sense already the numbered particles of loss we will shortly be assigned. When we say good night–the air is milder, spring now–we're reminded of our rapidly narrowed perspective. We hang on tighter to each other, since all we know of consequence tells us that we may not be this lavishly favored again.

Lately we've been working hard, preparing for our concert. This is what Madam Bessant calls it–a concert. A little program to end the term. Her suggestion, the first time she utters it–"We will end the season with a concert"–dumfounds us. An absurdity, an embarrassment. We are being asked to give a recital, to perform. Like trained seals or small children. Called upon to demonstrate our progress. Cecile Landreau's eyebrows go up in protest; her chin puckers the way it does when she launches into one of her picaresque western anecdotes. But no one says a word–how can we? Enigmatic, inconsolable Madam Bessant has offered up the notion of a concert. She has no idea of what we know, that the tragic narrative of her life has been laid bare. She speaks calmly, expectantly; she is innocence itself, never guessing how charged we are by our guilty knowledge, how responsible. The hazards of the grown-up life are settled on her face. We know everything about the Chopin nocturne, repeated and repeated, and about the stumbling collapse on the hot tracks, the severed head and bloodied torso. When she speaks of a concert we can only nod and agree. Of course there must be a concert.

It is decided then. We will do nine short pieces. Nothing too onerous though, the program must be kept light, entertaining.

And who is to be entertained? Madam Bessant patiently explains: we are to invite our friends, our families, and these *invitées* will form an audience for our concert. A *soirée*, she calls it now. Extra chairs have already been requisitioned, also a buffet table, and she herself–she brings her fingers and thumbs together to make a little diamond–she herself will provide refreshments.

This we won't hear of. Lonnie H. immediately volunteers a chocolate cake. Robert Mooney says to leave the wine to him, he knows a dealer. You insist on taking responsibility for a cheese and cold-cuts tray. Cecile and Rhonda will bring coffee, paper plates, plastic forks and knives. And Pierre and I, what do we bring?–potato chips, pretzels, nuts? Someone writes all this down, a list. Our final celebratory evening is to be orderly, apt, joyous, memorable.

Everyone knows the fourteenth of May in Montreal is a joke. It can be anything. You can have a blizzard or a heat wave. But that year, our year, it is a warm rainy night. A border of purple collects along the tops of the warehouses across the street from the

Y, and pools of oily violet shimmer on the rough pavement, tinted by the early night sky. Only Madam Bessant arrives with an umbrella; only Madam Bessant *owns* an umbrella. Spinning it vigorously, glancing around, setting it in a corner to dry. *Voilà*, she says, addressing it matter-of-factly, speaking also to the ceiling and partially opened windows.

We are all prompt except for Robert Mooney, who arrives a few minutes late with a carton of wine and with his wife on his arm–hooked there, hanging on tight. We see a thick girdled matron with square dentures and a shrub of bronze curls, dense as Brillo pads. Gravely, taking his time, he introduces her to us–"May I present Mrs. Mooney"–preserving the tender secret of her first name, and gently he leads her toward one of the folding chairs, arranging her cardigan around her shoulders as if she were an invalid. She settles in, handbag stowed on the floor, guarded on each side by powerful ankles. She has the hard compact head of a baby lion and a shy smile packed with teeth.

Only Robert Mooney has risked us to indifferent eyes. The rest of us bring no one. Madam Bessant's mouth goes into a worried circle and she casts an eye across the room where a quantity of food is already laid out on a trestle table. A cheerful paper table-cloth, bright red in color, has been spread. Also a surprise platter of baby shrimp and ham. Wedges of lemon straddle the shrimp. A hedge of parsley presses against the ham. About our absent guests, we're full of excuses, surprisingly similar–friends who canceled at the last minute, out-of-town emergencies, illness. Madam Bessant shrugs minutely, sighs, and looks at her watch. She is wearing a pink dress with large white dots. When eight o'clock comes she clears her throat and says, "I suppose we might as well go through our program anyway. It will be good practice for us, and perhaps Madam Mooney will bear with us."

Oh, we play beautifully, ingeniously, with a strict sense of ceremony, never more alert to our intersecting phrases and spelled out consonance. Lonnie H. plays with her eyes sealed shut, as though dreaming her way through a tranced lifetime, backward and also forward, extending outward, collapsing inward. Your foot does its circling journey, around and around, keeping order. Next to you is Robert Mooney whose face, as he puffs away, has grown rosy and tender, a little shy, embarrassed by his virtue, surprised by it too. Rhonda's forehead creases into that touching squint of hers. (You can be seduced by such intense looks of concentration; it's that rare.) Cecile's wrist darts forward, turning over the sheets, never missing a note, and Pierre's fingers move like water around his tricks of practiced tension and artful release.

And Mrs. Mooney, our audience of one, listens and nods, nods and listens, and then, after a few minutes, when we're well launched, leans down and pulls some darning from the brocade bag on the floor. A darkish tangle, a lapful of softness. She works away at it throughout our nine pieces. These must be Robert Mooney's socks she's mending, these long dark curls of wool wrapped around her left hand, so intimately stabbed by her darting needle. Her mouth is busy, wetting the thread, biting it off, full of knowledge. Between each of our pieces she looks up, surprised, opens her teeth and says in a good-natured, good-sport voice, "Perfectly lovely." At the end, after the conclusion has been signaled with an extra measure of silence, she stows the socks in the bag, pokes the needle resolutely away, smiles widely with her stretched mouth and begins to applaud.

Is there any sound so strange and brave and ungainly as a single person clapping in a room? All of us, even Madam Bessant, instinctively shrink from the rhythmic unevenness of it, and from the crucial difficulty of knowing when it will stop. If it ever does stop. The brocade bag slides off Mrs. Mooney's lap to the floor, but still she goes on applauding. The furious upward growth of her hair shimmers and so do the silver veins on the back of her hands. On and on she claps, powerless, it seems, to stop. We half rise, hover in mid-air, then resume our seats. At last Robert Mooney gets up, crosses the room to his wife and kisses her loudly on the lips. A smackeroo–the word comes to me on little jointed legs, an artifact from another era, out of a comic book. It breaks the spell. Mrs. Mooney looks up at her husband, her hard lion's head wrapped in surprise. "Lovely," she pronounces. "Absolutely lovely."

After that the evening winds down quickly. Rhonda gives a tearful rambling speech, reading from some notes she's got cupped in her hand, and presents Madam Bessant with a pair of earrings shaped, if I remember, like treble clefs. We have each put fifty cents or maybe a dollar toward these earrings, which Madam Bessant immediately puts on, dropping her old silver snails into her coin purse, closing it with a snap, her life beginning a sharp new chapter.

Of course there is too much food. We eat what we

can, though hardly anyone touches the shrimp, and
then divide between us the quantities of leftovers, a
spoiling surfeit that subtly discolors what's left of the
evening.

Robert and his wife take their leave. "Gotta get my
beauty sleep," he says loudly. He shakes our hands,
that little muscular fist, and wishes us luck. What
does he mean by luck? Luck with what? He says he's
worried about getting a parking ticket. He says his
wife gets tired, that her back acts up. "So long, gang,"
he says, backing out of the room and tripping slightly
on a music stand, his whole dark face screwed up
into what looks like an obscene wink of farewell.

Madam Bessant, however, doesn't notice. She turns
to us smiling, her odd abbreviated little teeth opening
to deliver a surprise. She has arranged for a different
baby sitter tonight. For once there's no need for her
to rush home. She's free to join us for an hour at Le
Piston. She smiles shyly; she knows, it seems, about
our after-class excursions, though how we can't
imagine.

But tonight Le Piston is closed temporarily for
renovations. We find the door locked. Brown wrapping paper has been taped across the windows. In
fact, when it opens some weeks later it has been
transformed into a produce market, and today it's a
second-hand bookshop specializing in mysteries.

Someone mentions another bar a few blocks away,
but Madam Bessant sighs at the suggestion; the sigh
comes spilling out of an inexpressible, segmented
exhaustion which none of us understands. She sighs
a second time, shifts her shopping bag loaded with
leftover food. The treble clefs seem to drag on her ear
lobes. Perhaps, she says, she should go straight home

after all. Something may have gone wrong. You can never know with children. Emergencies present themselves. She says good night to each of us in turn. There is some confusion, as though she has just this minute realized how many of us there are and what we are called. Then she walks briskly away from us in the direction of the Métro station.

The moment comes when we should exchange addresses and phone numbers or make plans to form a little practice group to meet on a monthly basis perhaps, maybe in the undeclared territory of our own homes, perhaps for the rest of our lives.

But it doesn't happen. The light does us in, the too-soft spring light. There's too much ease in it, it's too much like ordinary daylight. A drift of orange sun reaches us through a break in the buildings and lightly mocks our idea of finding another bar. It forbids absolutely a final embrace, and something nearer shame than embarrassment makes us anxious to end the evening quickly and go off in our separate directions.

Not forever, of course; we never would have believed that. Our lives at that time were a tissue of suspense with surprise around every corner. We would surely meet again, bump into each other in a restaurant or maybe even in another evening class. A thousand spontaneous meetings could be imagined.

It may happen yet. The past has a way of putting its tentacles around the present. You might–you, my darling, with your black tights and cough drops–you might feel an urge to write me a little note, a few words for the sake of nostalgia and nothing more. I picture the envelope waiting in my mailbox, the astonishment after all these years, the wonder that you tracked me down. Your letter would set into motion a chain of events–since the links between us all are finely sprung and continuous–and the very next day I might run into Pierre on St. Catherine's. What a shout of joy we'd give out, the two of us, after our initial amazement. That very evening a young woman, or perhaps not so very young, might rush up to me in the lobby of a concert hall: Lonnie H., quieter now, but instantly recognizable, that bush of orange hair untouched by gray. The next day I imagine the telephone ringing: Cecile or Rhonda–why not?

We would burrow our way back quickly to those winter nights, saying it's been too long, it's been too bad, saying how the postures of love don't really change. We could take possession of each other once again, conjure our old undisturbed, unquestioning chemistry. The wonder is that it hasn't already happened. You would think we made a pact never to meet again. You would think we put an end to it, just like that–saying good-bye to each other, and meaning it.

Hazel

After a man has mistreated a woman he feels a need to do something nice which she must accept.

In line with this way of thinking, Hazel has accepted from her husband, Brian, sprays of flowers, trips to Hawaii, extravagant compliments on her rather ordinary cooking, bracelets of dull-colored silver and copper, a dressing gown in green tartan wool, a second dressing gown with maribou trim around the hem and sleeves, dinners in expensive revolving restaurants and, once, a tender kiss, tenderly delivered, on the instep of her right foot.

But there will be no more such compensatory gifts, for Brian died last December of heart failure.

The heart failure, as Hazel, even after all these years, continues to think of it. In her family, the family of her girlhood that is, a time of gulped confusion in a place called Porcupine Falls, all familiar diseases were preceded by the horrific article: *the* measles, *the* polio, *the* rheumatism, *the* cancer, and–to come down to her husband Brian and his final thrashing with life–*the* heart failure.

He was only fifty-five. He combed his uncolored hair smooth and wore clothes made of gabardinelike materials, a silky exterior covering a complex core. It took him ten days to die after the initial attack, and during the time he lay there, all his minor wounds healed. He was a careless man who bumped into things, shrubbery, table legs, lighted cigarettes, simple curbstones. Even the making of love seemed to him a labor and a recovery, attended by scratches, bites, effort, exhaustion and, once or twice, a mild but humiliating infection. Nevertheless, women found him attractive. He had an unhurried, good-humored persistence about him and could be kind when he chose to be.

The night he died Hazel came home from the hospital and sat propped up in bed till four in the morning, reading a trashy, fast-moving New York novel about wives who lived in spacious duplexes overlooking Central Park, too alienated to carry on properly with their lives. They made salads with rare kinds of lettuce and sent their apparel to the dry cleaners, but they were bitter and helpless. Frequently they used the expression "fucked up" to describe their malaise. Their mothers or their fathers had fucked them up, or jealous sisters or bad-hearted nuns, but mainly they had been fucked up by men who no longer cared about them. These women were immobilized by the lack of love and kept alive only by a reflexive bounce between new ways of arranging salad greens and fantasies of suicide. Hazel wondered as she read how long it took for the remembered past to sink from view. A few miserable tears crept into her eyes, her first tears since Brian's initial attack, that shrill telephone call, that unearthly hour. Impetuously she wrote on the book's flyleaf the melodramatic words "I am alone and suffering unbearably." Not her best handwriting, not her usual floating morning-glory tendrils. Her fingers cramped at this hour. The cheap ball-point pen held back its ink, and the result was a barely legible scrawl that she nevertheless underlined twice.

By mid-January she had taken a job demonstrating kitchenware in department stores. The ad in the newspaper promised on-the-job training, opportunities for advancement and contact with the public. Hazel submitted to a short, vague, surprisingly painless interview, and was rewarded the following morning by a telephone call telling her she was to start immediately. She suspected she was the sole applicant, but nevertheless went numb with shock. Shock and also pleasure. She hugged the elbows of her dressing gown and smoothed the sleeves flat. She was fifty years old and without skills, a woman who had managed to avoid most of the arguments and issues of the world. Asked a direct question, her voice wavered. She understood nothing of the national debt or the situation in Nicaragua, nothing. At ten-thirty most mornings she was still in her dressing gown and had the sense to know this was shameful. She possessed a softened, tired body and rubbed-looking eyes. Her posture was only moderately good. She often touched her mouth with the back of her hand. Yet someone, some person with a downtown commercial address and an official letterhead and a firm telephone manner had seen fit to offer her a job.

Only Hazel, however, thought the job a good idea.

Brian's mother, a woman in her eighties living in a suburban retirement center called Silver Oaks, said, "Really, there is no need, Hazel. There's plenty of money if you live reasonably. You have your condo paid for, your car, a good fur coat that'll last for years. Then there's the insurance and Brian's pension, and when you're sixty-five–now don't laugh, sixty-five will come, it's not that far off–you'll have your social security. You have a first-rate lawyer to look after your investments. There's no need."

Hazel's closest friend, Maxine Forestadt, a woman of her own age, a demon bridge player, a divorcée, a woman with a pinkish powdery face loosened by too many evenings of soft drinks and potato chips and too much cigarette smoke flowing up toward her eyes, said, "Look. You're not the type, Hazel. Period. I know the type and you're not it. Believe me. All right, so you feel this urge to assert yourself, to try to prove something. I know, I went through it myself, wanting to show the world I wasn't just this dipsy pushover and hanger-oner. But this isn't for you, Haze, this eight-to-five purgatory, standing on your feet, and especially *your* feet, your arches, your arches act up just shopping. I know what you're trying to do, but in the long run, what's the point?"

Hazel's older daughter, Marilyn, a pathologist, and possibly a lesbian, living in a women's co-op in the east end of the city, phoned and, drawing on the sort of recollection that Hazel already had sutured, said,

"Dad would not have approved. I know it, you know it. I mean, Christ, flogging pots and pans, it's so public. People crowding around. Idle curiosity and greed, a free show, just hanging in for a teaspoon of bloody quiche lorraine or whatever's going. Freebies. People off the street, bums, anybody. Christ. Another thing, you'll have to get a whole new wardrobe for a job like that. Eye shadow so thick it's like someone's given you a punch. Just ask yourself what Dad would have said. I know what he would have said, he would have said thumbs down, nix on it."

Hazel's other daughter, Rosie, living in British Columbia, married to a journalist, wrote: "Dear Mom, I absolutely respect what you're doing and admire your courage. But Robin and I can't help wondering if you've given this decision enough thought. You remember how after the funeral, back at your place with Grandma and Auntie Maxine and Marilyn, we had that long talk about the need to lie fallow for a bit and not rush headlong into things and making major decisions, just letting the grieving process take its natural course. Now here it is, a mere six weeks later, and you've got yourself involved with these cookware people. I just hope you haven't signed anything. Robin says he never heard of Kitchen Kult and it certainly isn't listed on the boards. We're just anxious about you, that's all. And this business of working on commission is exploitative to say the least. Ask Marilyn. You've still got your shorthand and typing and, with a refresher course, you proba-bly could find something, maybe Office Overload would give you a sense of your own independence and some spending money besides. We just don't want to see you hurt, that's all."

At first, Hazel's working day went more or less like this: at seven-thirty her alarm went off; the first five minutes were the worst; such a steamroller of sorrow passed over her that she was left as flat and lifeless as the queen-size mattress that supported her. Her squashed limbs felt emptied of blood, her breath came out thin and cool and quiet as ether. What was she to do? How was she to live her life? She mouthed these questions to the silky blanket binding, rubbing her lips frantically back and forth across the stitching. Then she got up, showered, did her hair, made coffee and toast, took a vitamin pill, brushed her teeth, made up her face (going easy on the eye shadow), and put on her coat. By eight-thirty she was in her car and checking her city map.

Reading maps, the tiny print, the confusion, caused her headaches. And she had trouble with orientation, turning the map first this way, then that, never willing to believe that north must lie at the top. North's natural place should be toward the bottom, past the Armoury and stockyards where a large cold lake bathed the city edges. Once on a car trip to the Indian River country early in their married life, Brian had joked about her lack of map sense. He spoke happily of this failing, proudly, giving her arm a squeeze, and then had thumped the cushioned steering wheel. Hazel, thinking about the plushy thump, wished she hadn't. To recall something once was to remember it forever; this was something she had only recently discovered, and she felt that the discovery might be turned to use.

The Kitchen Kult demonstrations took her on a revolving cycle of twelve stores, some of them in corners of the city where she'd seldom ventured. The

Italian district. The Portuguese area. Chinatown. A young Kitchen Kult salesman named Peter Lemmon broke her in, *familiarizing* her as he put it with the Kitchen Kult product. He taught her the spiel, the patter, the importance of keeping eye contact with customers at all times, how to draw on the mood and size of the crowd and play, if possible, to its ethnic character, how to make Kitchen Kult products seem like large beautiful toys, easily mastered and guaranteed to win the love and admiration of friends and family.

"That's what people out there really want," Peter Lemmon told Hazel, who was surprised to hear this view put forward so undisguisedly. "Lots of love and truckloads of admiration. Keep that in mind. People can't get enough."

He had an aggressive pointed chin and ferocious red sideburns, and when he talked he held his lips together so that the words came out with a soft zitherlike slur. Hazel noticed his teeth were discolored and badly crowded, and she guessed that this accounted for his guarded way of talking. Either that or a nervous disposition. Early on, to put him at his ease, she told him of her small-town upbringing in Porcupine Falls, how her elderly parents had never quite recovered from the surprise of having a child. How at eighteen she came to Toronto to study stenography. That she was now a widow with two daughters, one of whom she suspected of being unhappily married and one who was undergoing a gender crisis. She told Peter Lemmon that this was her first real job, that at the age of fifty she was out working for the first time. She talked too much, babbled in fact–why? She didn't know. Later she was sorry.

In return he confided, opening his mouth a little wider, that he was planning to have extensive dental work in the future if he could scrape the money together. More than nine thousand dollars had been quoted. A quality job cost quality cash, that was the long and short of it, so why not take the plunge. He hoped to go right to the top with Kitchen Kult. Not just sales, but the real top, and that meant management. It was a company, he told her, with a forward-looking sales policy and sound product.

It disconcerted Hazel at first to hear Peter Lemmon speak of the Kitchen Kult product without its grammatical article, and she was jolted into the remembrance of how she had had to learn to suppress the article that attached to bodily ailments. When demonstrating product, Peter counseled, keep it well in view, repeating product's name frequently and withholding product's retail price until the actual demo and tasting has been concluded.

After two weeks Hazel was on her own, although Peter Lemmon continued to meet her at the appointed "sales venue" each morning, bringing with him in a company van the equipment to be demonstrated and helping her "set up" for the day. She slipped into her white smock, the same one every day, a smooth permapress blend with grommets down the front and Kitchen Kult in red script across the pocket, and stowed her pumps in a plastic bag, putting on the white crepe-soled shoes Peter Lemmon had recommended. "Your feet, Hazel, are your capital." He also produced, of his own volition, a tall collapsible stool on which she could perch in such a way that she appeared from across the counter to be standing unsupported.

She started each morning with a demonstration of the Jiffy-Sure-Slicer, Kitchen Kult's top seller, accounting for some sixty per cent of total sales. For an hour or more, talking to herself, or rather to the empty air, she shaved hillocks of carrots, beets, parsnips and rutabagas into baroque curls or else she transformed them into little star-shaped discs or elegant matchsticks. The use of cheap root vegetables kept the demo costs down, Peter Lemmon said, and presented a less threatening challenge to the average shopper, Mrs. Peas and Carrots, Mrs. Corn Niblets.

As Hazel warmed up, one or two shoppers drifted toward her, keeping her company—she learned she could count on these one or two who were elderly women for the most part, puffy of face and bulgy of eye. Widows, Hazel decided. The draggy-hemmed coats and beige tote bags gave them away. Like herself, though perhaps a few years older, these women had taken their toast and coffee early and had been driven out into the cold in search of diversion. "Just set the dial, ladies and gentlemen," Hazel told the discomfited two or three voyeurs, "and press gently on the Jiffy lever. Never requires sharpening, never rusts."

By mid-morning she generally had fifteen people gathered about her, by noon as many as forty. No one interrupted her, and why should they? She was free entertainment. They listened, they exchanged looks, they paid attention, they formed a miniature,

temporary colony of good will and consumer serious-
ness waiting to be instructed, initiated into Hazel's
rituals and promises.

At the beginning of her third week, going solo for
the first time, she looked up to see Maxine in her long
beaver coat, gawking. "Now this is just what you
need, madam," Hazel sang out, not missing a beat, an
uncontrollable smile on her face. "In no time you'll
be making more nutritious, appealing salads for your
family and friends and for those bridge club get-
togethers."

Maxine had been offended. She complained afterward to Hazel that she found it embarrassing being
picked out in a crowd like that. It was insulting,
especially to mention the bridge club as if she did
nothing all day long but shuffle cards. "It's a bit
thick, Hazel, especially when you used to enjoy a
good rubber yourself. And you know I only play
cards as a form of social relaxation. You used to enjoy
it, and don't try to tell me otherwise because I won't
buy it. We miss you, we really do. I know perfectly
well it's not easy for you facing Francine. She was
always a bit of a you-know-what, and Brian was, God
knows, susceptible, though I have to say you've put a
dignified face on the whole thing. I don't think I
could have done it, I don't have your knack for
looking the other way, never have had, which is why
I'm where I'm at, I suppose. But who are you really
cheating, dropping out of the bridge club like this? I
think, just between the two of us, that Francine's a
bit hurt, she thinks you hold her responsible for
Brian's attack, even though we all know that when
our time's up, it's up. And besides, it takes two."

In the afternoon, after a quick pick-up lunch (leftover grated raw vegetables usually or a hard-boiled egg), Hazel demonstrated Kitchen Kult's all-purpose non-stick fry pan. The same crowds that admired her julienne carrots seemed ready to be mesmerized by the absolute roundness of her crepes and omelets, their uniform gold edges and the ease with which they came pulling away at a touch of her spatula. During the early months, January, February, Hazel learned just how easily people could be hypnotized, how easily, in fact, they could be put to sleep. Their mouths sagged. They grew dull-eyed and immobile. Their hands went hard into their pockets. They hugged their purses tight.

Then one afternoon a small fortuitous accident occurred: a crepe, zealously flipped, landed on the floor. Because of the accident, Hazel discovered how a rupture in routine could be turned to her advantage. "Whoops-a-daisy," she said that first day, stooping to recover the crepe. People laughed out loud. It was as though Hazel's mild exclamation had a forgotten period fragrance to it. "I guess I don't know my own strength," she said, shaking her curls and earning a second ripple of laughter.

After that she began, at least once or twice a day, to misdirect a crepe. Or overcook an omelet. Or bring herself to a state of comic tears over her plate of chopped onions. "Not my day," she would croon. Or "good grief" or "sacred rattlesnakes" or a shrugging, cheerful, "who ever promised perfection on the first try." Some of the phrases that came out of her mouth reminded her of the way people talked in Porcupine Falls back in a time she could not possibly have remembered. Gentle, unalarming expletives calling up wells of good nature and neighborliness. She wouldn't have guessed she had this quality of rubbery humor inside her.

After a while she felt she could get away with anything as long as she kept up her line of chatter. That was the secret, she saw—never to stop talking. That was why these crowds gave her their attention: she could perform miracles (with occasional calculated human lapses) and keep right on talking at the same time. Words, a river of words. She had never before talked at such length, as though she were driving a wedge of air ahead of her. It was easy, *easy*. She dealt out repetitions, little punchy pushes of emphasis, and an ever growing inventory of affectionate declarations directed toward her vegetable friends. "What a devil!" she said, holding aloft a head of bulky cauliflower. "You darling radish, you !" She felt foolish at times, but often exuberant, like a semi-retired, slightly eccentric actress. And she felt, oddly, that she was exactly as strong and clever as she need be.

But the work was exhausting. She admitted it. Every day the crowds had to be wooed afresh. By five-thirty she was too tired to do anything more than drive home, make a sandwich, read the paper, rinse out her Kitchen Kult smock and hang it over the shower rail, then get into bed with a thick paperback. Propped up in bed reading, her book like a wimple at her chin, she seemed to have flames on her feet and on the tips of her fingers, as though she'd burned her way through a long blur of a day and now would burn the night behind her too.

January, February, the first three weeks of March. So this was what work was: a two-way bargain people made with the world, a way to reduce time to rubble.

The books she read worked braids of panic into her consciousness. She'd drifted toward historical fiction, away from Central Park and into the Regency courts of England. But were the queens and courtesans any happier than the frustrated New York wives? Were they less lonely, less adrift? So far she had found no evidence of it. They wanted the same things more or less: abiding affection, attention paid to their moods and passing thoughts, their backs rubbed and, now and then, the tender grateful application of hands and lips. She remembered Brian's back turned toward her in sleep, well covered with flesh in his middle years. He had never been one for pajamas, and she had often been moved to reach out and stroke the smooth mound of flesh. She had not found his extra weight disagreeable, far from it.

In Brian's place there remained now only the rectangular softness of his allergy-free pillow. Its smooth casing, faintly puckered at the corners, had the feel of mysterious absence.

"But why does it always have to be one of my *friends!*" she had cried out at him once at the end of a long quarrel. "Don't you see how humiliating it is for me?"

He had seemed genuinely taken aback, and she saw in a flash it was only laziness on his part, not express cruelty. She recalled his solemn promises, his wet eyes, new beginnings. She fondly recalled, too, the resonant pulmonary sounds of his night breathing, the steep climb to the top of each inhalation and the tottery stillness before the descent. How he used to lull her to sleep with this nightly music! Compensations. But she had not asked for enough, hadn't known what to ask for, what was owed her.

It was because of the books she read, their dense complications and sharp surprises, that she had applied for a job in the first place. She had a sense of her own life turning over page by page, first a girl, then a young woman, then married with two young daughters, then a member of a bridge club and a quilting club, and now, too soon for symmetry, a widow. All of it fell into small childish paragraphs, the print over-large and blocky like a school reader. She had tried to imagine various new endings or turnings for herself–she might take a trip around the world or sign up for a course in ceramics–but could think of nothing big enough to fill the vacant time left to her–except perhaps an actual job. This was what other people did, tucking in around the edges those little routines–laundry, meals, errands–that had made up her whole existence.

"You're wearing yourself out," Brian's mother said when Hazel arrived for an Easter Sunday visit, bringing with her a double-layered box of chocolate almond bark and a bouquet of tulips. "Tearing all over town every day, on your feet, no proper lunch arrangements. You'd think they'd give you a good hour off and maybe a lunch voucher, give you a chance to catch your breath. It's hard on the back, standing. I always feel my tension in my back. These are delicious, Hazel, not that I'll eat half of them, not with my appetite, but it'll be something to pass round to the other ladies. Everyone shares here, that's one thing. And the flowers, tulips! One or the other would

have more than sufficed, Hazel, you've been extravagant. I suppose now that you're actually earning, it
makes a difference. You feel differently, I suppose,
when it's your own money. Brian's father always saw
that I had everything I needed, wanted for nothing,
but I wouldn't have minded a little money of my
own, though I never said so, not in so many
words."

One morning Peter Lemmon surprised Hazel, and
frightened her too, by saying, "Mr. Cortland wants to
see you. The big boss himself. Tomorrow at ten-
thirty. Downtown office. Headquarters. I'll cover the
venue for you."

Mr. Cortland was the age of Hazel's son-in-law,
Robin. She couldn't have said why, but she had
expected someone theatrical and rude, not this handsome curly-haired man unwinding himself from
behind a desk that was not really a desk but a
gate-legged table, shaking her hand respectfully and
leading her toward a soft brown easy chair. There
was genuine solemnity to his jutting chin and a thick
brush of hair across his quizzing brow. He offered her
a cup of coffee. "Or perhaps you would prefer tea,"
he said, very politely, with a shock of inspiration.

She looked up from her shoes, her good polished
pumps, not her nurse shoes, and saw a pink conch
shell on Mr. Cortland's desk. It occurred to her it
must be one of the things that made him happy.
Other people were made happy by music or flowers
or bowls of ice cream–enchanted, familiar things.
Some people collected china, and when they found a
long-sought piece, *that* made them happy. What
made *her* happy was the obliteration of time, burning it away so cleanly she hardly noticed it. Not that

she said so to Mr. Cortland. She said, in fact, very little, though some dragging filament of intuition urged her to accept tea rather than coffee, to forgo milk, to shake her head sadly over the proffered sugar.

"We are more delighted than I can say with your sales performance," Mr. Cortland said. "We are a small but growing firm and, as you know"–Hazel did not know, how could she?–"we are a family concern. My maternal grandfather studied commerce at McGill and started this business as a kind of hobby. Our aim, the family's aim, is a reliable product, but not a hard sell. I can't stress this enough to our sales people. We are anxious to avoid a crude hectoring approach or tactics that are in any way manipulative, and we are in the process of developing a quality sales force that matches the quality of our product line. This may surprise you, but it is difficult to find people like yourself who possess, if I may say so, your gentleness of manner. People like yourself transmit a sense of trust to the consumer. We've heard very fine things about you, and we have decided, Hazel–I do hope I may call you Hazel–to put you on regular salary, in addition of course to an adjusted commission. And I would like also to present you with this small brooch, a glazed ceramic K for Kitchen Kult, which we give each quarter to our top sales person."

"Do you realize what this means?" Peter Lemmon asked later that afternoon over a celebratory drink at Mr. Duck's Happy Hour. "Salary means you're on the team, you're a Kitchen Kult player. Salary equals professional, Hazel. You've arrived, and I don't think you even realize it."

Hazel thought she saw flickering across Peter's guarded, eager face, like a blade of sunlight through a thick curtain, the suggestion that some privilege had been carelessly allocated. She pinned the brooch on the lapel of her good spring coat with an air of bafflement. Beyond the simple smoothness of her pay check, she perceived dark squadrons of planners and decision makers who had brought this teasing irony forward. She was being rewarded–a bewildering turn of events–for her timidity, her self-efface-ment, for what Maxine called her knack for looking the other way. She was a shy, ineffectual, untrained, neutral looking woman, and for this she was being kicked upstairs, or at least this was how Peter translated her move from commission to salary. He scratched his neck, took a long drink of his beer, and said it a third time, with a touch of belligerence it seemed to Hazel, "a kick upstairs." He insisted on paying for the drinks, even though Hazel pressed a ten-dollar bill into his hand. He shook it off.

"This place is bargain city," he assured her, open-ing the orange cave of his mouth, then closing it quickly. He came here often after work, he said, taking advantage of the two-for-one happy hour policy. Not that he was tight with his money, just the opposite, but he was setting aside a few dollars a week for his dental work in the summer. The work was mostly cosmetic, caps and spacers, and therefore not covered by Kitchen Kult's insurance scheme. The way he saw it, though, was as an investment in the future. If you were going to go to the top, you had to be able to open your mouth and project. "Like this brooch, Hazel, it's a way of projecting. Wearing the company logo means you're one of the family and that you don't mind shouting it out."

That night, when she whitened her shoes, she felt a sort of love for them. And she loved, too, suddenly, her other small tasks, rinsing out her smock, setting her alarm, settling into bed with her book, resting her head against Brian's little fiber-filled pillow with its stitched remnant of erotic privilege and reading herself out of her own life, leaving behind her cut-out shape, so bulky, rounded and unimaginably mute, a woman who swallowed her tongue, got it jammed down her throat and couldn't make a sound.

Marilyn gave a shout of derision on seeing the company brooch pinned to her mother's raincoat. "The old butter-up trick. A stroke here, a stroke there, just enough to keep you going and keep you grateful. But at least they had the decency to get you off straight commission, for that I have to give them some credit."

"Dear Mother," Rosie wrote from British Columbia. "Many thanks for the waterless veg cooker which is surprisingly well made and really very attractive too, and Robin feels that it fulfills a real need, nutritionally speaking, and also aesthetically."

"You're looking better," Maxine said. "You look as though you've dropped a few pounds, have you? All those grated carrots. But do you ever get a minute to yourself? Eight hours on the job plus commuting. I don't suppose they even pay for your gas, which adds up, and your parking. You want to think about a holiday, people can't be buying pots and pans three hundred and sixty-five days a year. JoAnn and Francine and I are thinking seriously of getting a cottage in Nova Scotia for two weeks. Let me know if you're interested, just tell those Kitchen Kult moguls you owe yourself a little peace and quiet by the seaside, ha! Though you do look more relaxed than the last time I saw you, you looked wrung out, completely."

In early May Hazel had an accident. She and Peter were setting up one morning, arranging a new demonstration, employing the usual cabbage, beets and onions, but adding a few spears of spring asparagus and a scatter of chopped chives. In the interest of economy she'd decided to split the asparagus lengthwise, bringing her knife first through the tender tapered head and down the woody stem. Peter was talking away about a new suit he was thinking of buying, asking Hazel's advice–should he go all out for a fine summer wool or compromise on wool and viscose? The knife slipped and entered the web of flesh between Hazel's thumb and forefinger. It sliced further into the flesh than she would have believed possible, so quickly, so lightly that she could only gaze at the spreading blood and grieve about the way it stained and spoiled her perfect circle of cucumber slices.

She required twelve stitches and, at Peter's urging, took the rest of the day off. Mr. Cortland's secretary telephoned and told her to take the whole week off if necessary. There were insurance forms to sign, but those could wait. The important thing was–but Hazel couldn't remember what the important thing was; she had been given some painkillers at the hospital and was having difficulty staying awake. She slept the afternoon away, dreaming of green fields and a yellow sun, and would have slept all evening too if she hadn't been wakened around eight o'clock by the faint buzz of her doorbell. She pulled on a dressing gown, a new one in flowered seersucker, and went to the door. It was Peter Lemmon with a clutch of flowers in his hand. "Why Peter," she said, and could think of nothing else.

The pain had left her hand and moved to the thin skin of her scalp. Its remoteness as much as its taut bright shine left her confused. She managed to take Peter's light jacket–though he protested, saying he had only come for a moment–and steered him toward a comfortable chair by the window. She listened as the cushions subsided under him, and hurried to put the flowers, already a little limp, into water, and to offer a drink–but what did she have on hand? No beer, no gin, and she knew better than to suggest sherry. Then the thought came: what about a glass of red wine?

He accepted twitchily. He said, "You don't have to twist my arm."

"You'll have to uncork it," Hazel said, gesturing at her bandaged hand. She felt she could see straight into his brain where there was nothing but rags and old plastic. But where had *this* come from, this sly, unpardonable superiority of hers?

He lurched forward, nearly falling. "Always happy to do the honors." He seemed afraid of her, of her apartment with its settled furniture, lamps and end tables and china cabinet, regarding these things first with a strict, dry, inquiring look. After a few minutes, he resettled in the soft chair with exaggerated respect.

"To your career," Peter said, raising his glass, appearing not to notice how the word career entered

Hazel's consciousness, waking her up from her haze of painkillers and making her want to laugh.

"To the glory of Kitchen Kult," she said, suddenly reckless. She watched him, or part of herself watched him, as he twirled the glass and sniffed its contents. She braced herself for what would surely come.

"An excellent vin–" he started to say, but was interrupted by the doorbell.

It was only Marilyn, dropping in as she sometimes did after her self-defense course. "Already I can break a collarbone," she told Peter after a flustered introduction, "and next week we're going to learn how to go for the groin."

She looked surprisingly pretty with her pensive, wet, youthful eyes and dusty lashes. She accepted some wine and listened intently to the story of Hazel's accident, then said, "Now listen, Mother, don't sign a release with Kitchen Kult until I have Edna look at it. You remember Edna, she's the lawyer. She's sharp as a knife; she's the one who did our lease for us, and it's airtight. You could develop blood poisoning or an infection, you can't tell at this point. You can't trust these corporate entities when it comes to–"

"Kitchen Kult," Peter said, twirling his glass in a manner Hazel found silly, "is more like a family."

"Balls."

"We've decided," Maxine told Hazel a few weeks later, "against the cottage in Nova Scotia. It's too risky, and the weather's only so-so according to Francine. And the cost of air fare and then renting a car, we just figured it's too expensive. My rent's going up starting in July and, well, I took a look at my bank balance and said, Maxine kid, you've got to tighten the old belt. As a matter of fact, I thought–now this may surprise you–I'm thinking of looking for a job."

Hazel set up an interview for Maxine through Personnel, and in a week's time Maxine did her first demonstration. Hazel helped break her in. As a result of a dimly perceived office shuffle, she had been promoted to Assistant Area Manager, freeing Peter Lemmon for what was described as "Creative Sales Outreach." The promotion worried her slightly and she wondered if she were being compensated for the nerve damage in her hand, which was beginning to look more or less permanent. "Thank God you didn't sign the release," was all Marilyn said.

"Congrats," Rosie wired from British Columbia after hearing about the promotion. Hazel had not received a telegram for some years. She was surprised that this austere printed sheet went by the name of telegram. Where was the rough gray paper and the little pasted together words? She wondered who had composed the message, Robin or Rosie, and whose idea it had been to abbreviate the single word and if thrift were involved. *Congrats.* What a hard little hurting pellet to find in the middle of a smooth sheet of paper.

"Gorgeous," Brian's mother said of Hazel's opal-toned silk suit with its scarf of muted pink, pearl and lemon. Her lips moved appreciatively. "Ah, gorgeous."

"A helluva improvement over a bloody smock," Maxine sniffed, looking sideways.

"Most elegant!" said Mr. Cortland, who had called Hazel into his office to discuss her future with Kitchen Kult. "The sort of image we hope and try to project. Elegance and understatement." He presented her with a small box in which rested, on a square of textured cotton, a pair of enameled earrings with the flying letter K for Kitchen Kult.

"Beautiful," said Hazel, who never wore earrings. The clip-on sort hurt her, and she had never got around to piercing her ears. "For my sake," Brian had begged her when he was twenty-five and she was twenty and about to become his wife, "don't ever do it. I can't bear to lose a single bit of you."

Remembering this, the tone of Brian's voice, its rushing, foolish sincerity, Hazel felt her eyes tingle. "My handbag," she said, groping blindly.

Mr. Cortland misunderstood. He leaped up, touched by his own generosity, a Kleenex in hand. "We simply wanted to show our appreciation," he said, or rather sang.

Hazel sniffed, more loudly than she intended, and Mr. Cortland pretended not to hear. "We especially appreciate your filling in for Peter Lemmon during his leave of absence."

At this Hazel nodded. Poor Peter. She must phone tonight. He was finding the aftermath of his dental surgery painful and prolonged, and she had been looking, every chance she had, for a suitable convalescent card, something not too effusive and not too mocking–Peter took his teeth far too seriously. Perhaps she would just send one of her blurry impressionistic hasty notes, or better yet, a jaunty postcard saying she hoped he'd be back soon.

Mr. Cortland fingered the pink conch shell on his desk. He picked it up between his two hands and rocked it gently to and fro, then said, "Mr. Lemmon will not be returning. We have already sent him a letter of termination and, of course, a generous severance settlement. It was decided that his particular kind of personality, though admirable, was not quite in line with the Kitchen Kult approach, and we feel that you yourself have already demonstrated your ability to take over his work and perhaps even extend the scope of it."

"I don't believe you're doing this," Marilyn shouted over the phone to Hazel. "And Peter doesn't believe it either."

"How do you know what Peter thinks?"

"I saw him this afternoon. I saw him yesterday afternoon. I see him rather often if you want to know the truth."

Hazel offered the Kitchen Kult earrings to Maxine who snorted and said, "Come off it, Hazel."

Rosie in Vancouver sent a short note saying, "Marilyn phoned about your new position, which is really marvelous, though Robin and I are wondering if you aren't getting in deeper than you really want to at this time."

Brian's mother said nothing. A series of small strokes had taken her speech away and also her ability to leave her bed. Nothing Hazel brought her aroused her interest, not chocolates, not flowers, not even the fashion magazines she used to love.

Hazel phoned and made an appointment to see Mr. Cortland. She invented a pretext, one or two ideas she and Maxine had worked out to tighten up the demonstrations. Mr. Cortland listened to her and nodded approvingly. Then she sprang. She had been thinking about Peter Lemmon, she said, how much

the sales force missed him, missed his resourceful-
ness and his attention to details. He had a certain
imaginative flair, a peculiar usefulness. Some people
had a way of giving energy to others, it was uncanny,
it was a rare gift. She didn't mention Peter's dental
work; she had some sense.

Mr. Cortland sent her a shrewd look, a look she
would not have believed he had in his repertoire.
"Well, Hazel," he said at last, "in business we deal in
hard bargains. Maybe you and I can come to some
sort of bargain."

"Bargain?"

"That insurance form, the release. The one you
haven't got round to signing yet. How would it be if
you signed it right now on the promise that I find
some slot or other for Peter Lemmon by the end of
the week? You are quite right about his positive
attributes, quite astute of you, really, to point them
out. I can't promise anything in sales though. The
absolute bottom end of management might be the
best we can do."

Hazel considered. She stared at the conch shell for
a full ten seconds. The office lighting coated it with a
pink, even light, making it look like a piece of
unglazed pottery. She liked the idea of bargains. She
felt she understood them. "I'll sign," she said. She
had her pen in her hand, poised.

On Sunday, a Sunday at the height of summer in
early July, Hazel drives out to Silver Oaks to visit her
ailing mother-in-law. All she can do for her now is sit
by her side for an hour and hold her hand, and
sometimes she wonders what the point is of these
visits. Her mother-in-law's face is impassive and
silken, and occasionally driblets of spittle, thin and

clear as tears, run from the corners of her mouth. It used to be such a strong, organized face with its firm mouth and steady eyes. But now she doesn't recognize anyone, with the possible exception of Hazel.

Some benefit appears to derive from these hand-holding sessions, or so the nurses tell Hazel. "She's calmer after your visits," they say. "She struggles less."

Hazel is calm too. She likes sitting here and feeling the hour unwind like thread from a spindle. She wishes it would go on and on. A week ago she had come away from Mr. Cortland's office irradiated with the conviction that her life was going to be possible after all. All she had to do was bear in mind the bargains she made. This was an obscene revelation, but Hazel was excited by it. Everything could be made accountable, added up and balanced and fairly, evenly, shared. You only had to pay attention and ask for what was yours by right. You could be clever, dealing in sly acts of surrender, but holding fast at the same time, negotiating and measuring and tying up your life in useful bundles.

But she was wrong. It wasn't true. Her pride had misled her. No one has that kind of power, no one.

She looks around the little hospital room and marvels at the accident of its contents, its bureau and tumbler and toothbrush and folded towel. The open window looks out on to a parking lot filled with rows of cars, all their shining roofs baking in the light. Next year there will be different cars, differently ordered. The shrubs and trees, weighed down with their millions of new leaves, will form a new dark backdrop.

It is an accident that she should be sitting in this

room, holding the hand of an old, unblinking, unre-
sisting woman who had once been sternly disapproving of her, thinking her countrified and clumsy.
"Hazel!" she had sometimes whispered in the early
days. "Your slip strap! Your salad fork!" Now she
lacks even the power to wet her lips with her tongue;
it is Hazel who touches the lips with a damp towel
from time to time, or applies a bit of Vaseline to keep
them from cracking. But she can feel the old
woman's dim pulse, and imagines that it forms a code
of acknowledgment or faintly telegraphs certain
perplexing final questions–how did all this happen?
How did we get here?

Everything is an accident, Hazel would be willing
to say if asked. Her whole life is an accident, and by
accident she has blundered into the heart of it.

Today Is the Day

Today is the day the women of our village go out along the highway planting blisterlilies. They set off without breakfast, not even coffee, gathering at the site of the old well, now paved over and turned into a tot lot and basketball court. The air at this hour is clear. You can breathe in the freshness. And you can smell the moist ground down there below the trampled weeds and baked clay, those eager black glinting minerals waiting, and the pocketed humus. A September morning. A thousand diamond points of dew.

The women carry small spades or else trowels. They talk quietly to each other, but in a murmuring way so that you can't make out the words; all you hear is a sound like cold water continuously falling, as if a faucet were left running into a large and heavy washtub.

At one time the blisterlily grew profusely on its own. By mid-May the shores of the two major lakes in the area were splashed with white, and the slopes leading up to the woods ablaze. It must have been a beautiful, compelling sight, although a single blister blossom is nothing spectacular. It springs up close to the ground like a crocus, its toothed cup of petals demurely white or faintly purple. The small, pointed, pale leaves are equally unprepossessing. By ones or twos the plant is more or less invisible. You'd step right on it if you weren't warned, crush it without knowing. It takes several million of the tiny blister-lily flowers to make an impact. And once, according to the old people of the village, there really were millions.

No one knows for sure what happened. Too much rain or not enough, that's one theory. Or something poisonous in the sunlight, radiation maybe, from the nearby power plant. Or earth tremors. Or insect pests. Or a drop in the annual mean temperature. All sorts and manner of explanations have been put forward: a vicious fungus of the sort that attacks common potatoes or a newly evolved, unkillable virus. Also mentioned is crowding by larger, more aggressive species such as the distantly related blue-wort, or the towering caster plant with its prickly seed pods, or the triple-spotted tigerleaf. There is only so much root room available at the earth's surface, and the root, or bulb rather, of the blisterlily is markedly acquiescent. To the eye it may look firm and reliable, an oval of slippery pearl under a loose russety skin, like a smallish onion or a French shallot, but it is actually soft-fleshed and far too obliging for its own good. Under even minimal pressure it shrivels or blisters and loses moisture, that much is known.

All the women of the village take part in the fall planting, including of course scrawny old Sally Bakey. Dirty, wearing a torn pinafore, less than four feet in height, it is Sally who discovered a new preserve of virgin blisterlilies in a meadow on the other side of the shiny westward-lying lake. There, where only mice walk, the flowers still grow in profusion, and the bulbs divide year by year as they once did in these parts.

Sally lives alone in a rough cabin on a diet of rolled oats and eggs. Raw eggs, some say. She has a foul smell and shouts obscenely at passers-by, especially those who betray by their manner of speech or dress that they are not of the region. But people like her smile. A troll's smile without teeth. In winter, when the snow reaches a certain height, the men of the village take its measure by saying: The snow's up to Sally Bakey's knees. Or over Sally Bakey's bum. Or clear up to Sally Bakey's eyebrows. No one knows how old Sally Bakey is, but she's old enough to remember when churches in the area were left unlocked and when people could go about knocking on any door and ask for a chair to sit down on or for a cup of strong tea.

From the railway bridge you can see the women fanned out along the highway in groups of twos or threes. Some of them work along the verge and others on the median. Right up to the horizon they go. In this part of the country, because the land is low lying and the sun reluctant, the horizon exercises an exceptionally strong influence. It presses downward like a punishing lintel. Every inch of pasture or woodland feels its weight, but roofs and chimneys and porches take the brunt of it, making the houses look squashed and stupid, thick-walled and inhospitable. It never lets up. But today the women, bending and patting their bulbs into place, then standing upright and placing their hands on their hips, taking a moment's rest, bring about a softening of the harsh horizontals. They scatter the light and, from a certain distance, the flexed silver of their bodies appears to pin the dark ground to the lowering sky, the way tablecloths and sheets are pinned to a slackly hung clothesline. There's ease in it, and merriment. Sally Bakey can be heard singing in her crone's cracked voice, a song she invents as she goes along–except for the refrain that is full of ritual cunning and defiance.

The women wear comfortable, practical clothes that are widely dissimilar in style and variously colored. Bright sports clothes. Fringed deerskin. Pants wide and narrow, reaching to the thigh, knee or ankle. Pleated skirts, leather tunics. Rayon blouses. Knitted cardigans. Aprons of terry cloth or linen. Dresses of denim, challis or finely shirred woven cotton. Age and inclination account for these differences.

Those women who are married have removed their wedding rings, and these rings are strung like beads on a length of common kitchen string that is securely knotted to form a necklace. This necklace or wreath or garland, whatever you choose to call it, has been attached to a low branch of a particular blue beech tree–not at all a common tree in the region–situated on a knoll of land north of the overpass. All day long, while the women bury the blisterlilies in the ground, this ring of gold shines in the open air, forming an almost perfect parabolic curve. Birds dive at it, puzzled. Spiders creep on its ridged surfaces and attempt to wrap it with webs. Often they succeed. The younger unmarried girls, happening near it, glance shyly in its direction, imagining its compounded weight and how it would feel to slip such a necklace over their heads. Unthinkable; even the strongest breezes barely manage to stir it.

The midday meal is taken in the shade of a birch grove, a favored spot. Birches are clean, kindly trees, particularly at this time of year, early fall, with the leaves not quite ready to let go, but thinned down to a soft old chamoislike dryness. There's plenty of room between the trees for the women to spread their blankets, and around the edges of these blankets they sit, talking, eating, with their legs tucked up under them. Everyone brings something, sandwiches, roasted chicken, raw vegetables and flasks of ice water or hot tea. The meal ends with dried apricots, eaten out of the hand like candy. Every year it is the youngest girls who take turns passing the apricots–Sally Bakey is served first–carrying them in a very old wooden bowl that has acquired a deep nutmeggy burnish over time. Some of the women reach up and stroke the slightly irregular sides of the bowl with their fingers, exclaiming over its durability and beauty.

The planting of the blisterlily continues until late afternoon. Between the red-stemmed alder bushes and Indian paintbrush, wild carrot, toadflax, spotted dock, milkweed, Michaelmas daisies, blue chickory, and stands of rare turtlehead lie thousands of newly nested blisterlily bulbs. A few good inches of black soil have been packed on top, enough to give protection through the winter months–seven months in all, for nothing will be seen of the blisterlily until the first week of May, perhaps later if the winter is particularly severe, perhaps not at all if things go badly.

The women, dispersing at the end of the day, resettle their rings on their fingers. Since morning they have been speaking in the old secret language of which, sadly, only eight verbs and some twenty nouns remain–but these they string together inventively, weaving a stratagem of potent suggestion overlain by a wily, votive grammar of sign and silence.

Now they revert to their common tongue and set off for home. Despite their fatigue they go on foot. They feel a chill breeze, notice a graying of the air, field stubble burning somewhere not far off. All that is ordinary and extraordinary about the day converges the minute they cross their separate thresholds. Necessity and order rush together, providing a tent of calm while they go about preparing the simplest of suppers, envelopes of soup and soda crackers, or plain bread and jam.

Sally Bakey, brewing her solitary tea, has an attack of the yawns. She's tired, more tired than anyone who knows her would believe. Shadows move on the wall behind her. Her old bones complain, whimper, and her yawning shades away into an unconscious sifting of images, one burning into another, stubborn and curious. An onion trying to be a flower. A long sleep in the frozen ground. Misgivings. Dread. Unbearable pressure. Cracked earth. The first small faintly colored shoot, surprised by its upright shadow. A hard round waxy bud. Watchfulness. More than watchfulness, a strict and willing observance.

Hinterland

Everyone seems to have stayed put this year except Meg and Roy Sloan of Milwaukee, Wisconsin.

Although both Meg and Roy are patriotic in a vague and non-rhetorical way, and good mature citizens who pay their taxes and vote and hold opinions on gun legislation and abortion, they've chosen this year to ignore the exhortation of their president to stay home and see America first. The Grand Canyon can wait, Roy says in the sociable weekend voice he more and more distrusts. The Black Hills can wait. And the Everglades. And Chesapeake Bay.

And they can wait forever, he privately thinks–with their slopes and depressions and fissured rock and silence and stubborn glare. He and Meg have come this fine golden September, now turned gray, but an endurable gray, to the city of Paris, and have settled down for three weeks in a small hotel near the Place Ferdinand, determined for once to do the thing right.

For the first ten days the sun gives out a soft powdery haze. Then it starts raining, little whips of water dashing down. Beneath their hotel window the streets are stripped of their elongated shadows and stippled light; this is suddenly a differently ordered reality, foreign and purposeful, with a harsh workaday existence and citizens so bound to their routines that they scarcely notice the serious, slightly older, end-of-season tourists, like the Sloans, who are taking in the sights.

Over the years, in the seasonal rounds of business and pleasure and special anniversaries, Meg and Roy Sloan have set foot on most of the continents of the world: Asia, Australia, South America–and of course Europe. They have, in fact, been to Paris on two previous occasions: for a single night in 1956, early April, their honeymoon, passing through on their way to Rome; and three days in 1967, an exhausting, hedonistic, aggressive survey that embraced the Moulin Rouge and the Jeu de Paume, Montmartre and Notre Dame, the Comédie Française and Malmaison, and that terminated with the rich, suppressed shame of a dinner in the Rue Royale where they suffered a contemptuous waiter, a wobbly table, scanty servings, and a yellow-eyed madam guarding the *toilette* and demanding payment of Meg–who pretended not to understand–and who muttered fiercely into her saucer of coins, *ça commence, ça commence*, meaning Meg Sloan of Milwaukee and the tidal wave of penny-pinching tourists who would follow, the affluent poor, the educationally driven, budget-bound North Americans whom Europeans so resemble but refuse to acknowledge.

And now, in the autumn of 1986, an uneasy, untrustful time in the world's history, the Sloans have returned.

"But why?" quite a number of their friends said. "Why Paris of all places!"

Meg Sloan is a small, dark, intense woman who, though not Jewish, might easily be thought to be. In any case, it seemed that Americans were singled out by terrorists, regardless of their background: bearded soft-spoken journalists taken hostage, nuns beaten and raped, a harmless old man pushed about and then shot, innocent children propelled through the suddenly gaping side of an aircraft. Why take needless risks, the Sloans' friends said. Why go out of your way to invite disaster? Furthermore the dollar had taken a rough punch, and you could get better nouvelle cuisine anyway right in Milwaukee, or at least Chicago, and not have to put up with people who were rude and unprincipled–remember that Greenpeace business last summer, still unresolved–besides which, three weeks devoted just to Paris seemed a lot when there was all of Europe to get a feel for.

"We're fatalists," Meg had countered, "and besides, we don't want to live out of a suitcase. Roy and I want to unpack for a change. You know, put our underwear in those big deep dresser drawers they have over there and actually hang up our clothes in one of those gorgeous armoire affairs and come back after a day of sightseeing and get into a bed we can depend on."

"What we'd really like," Roy said, "is to see how the true Parisians live."

In fact, he holds out little hope of this happening. At age fifty-five, the ability to penetrate and explore has left him, perhaps only temporarily–he hopes so. Mainly, as he sees it, he's forgotten how to pay attention, grown somehow incapacitated and lazy. At times he can't believe his own laziness. He chides himself, his sins of omission. He is a man so lazy, so remiss, he couldn't be bothered last spring to step into his own back yard for a glimpse of Halley's Comet. Halley's Comet won't come again, not in his lifetime–he knows this perfectly well. Unforgivable. Incomprehensible. What is the matter with him?

Both he and Meg were in need of a vacation. The long hot summer of patriotic excess at home had left him with what seemed like a bad case of flu, with aching muscles and slow settling fevers. His head felt stuffed with mineral whiteness: too many fireworks, too many hours before a TV set regarding the costly clamor over "Lady Liberty"–the epithet drummed hard on the lining of his skull. Who are these buoyant children anyway, he asked himself, addressing the black windows of his living room, and by what power had they turned him peevish and dull and out of tune with his own instincts?

There were other problems too. The Sloans' daughter Jenny had separated from her husband Kenneth for reasons not yet fully explained, and returned to the family home, bringing with her from Green Bay her two small children whose presence had unbalanced the house. Meg's nerves flared up overnight, her old insomnia came back, her eyes grew dry and jittery. Mother and daughter under one roof–the old,

old story, which neither of them would have credited, and each too tactful to overstep the other, each so protective of him, Roy (father, husband) that he was continually off-balance and awaiting an explosion that he doubted would ever come.

Then the idea of a vacation presented itself, getting away, the travel agent's mystic croon–a brief respite. A trip, a holiday. Escape. And it seemed, after some initial dithering, the thing to do. September was the worst possible time of the year for Roy to get away, but arrangements could always be–and were–worked out, and he and Meg were free to go anywhere within reason; for some time now money has not really been a hindrance.

They know, though, how to travel thriftily, how to save their receipts and write off what they can as professional expenses. Meg Sloan, for the last ten years or so, has made hand-painted, one-of-a-kind greeting cards, whimsical lines and squiggles on squares of rag paper that retail for five dollars apiece, and she has come to see her trips as opportunities to scout out new ideas. Roy Sloan, who heads a technical college in downtown Milwaukee, makes solemn, uncomfortable forays to similar institutions when traveling abroad, keeping notes on curriculum and entrance requirements and capital costs. These tax write-offs serve as an enabling tactic since both Roy and Meg grew up in frugal midwestern families and require the assurance that things are not as costly as they appear.

Certainly Paris is far from cheap. Their hotel is small, twenty rooms in all, and inconspicuous, but charges five hundred francs a night, which is one hundred dollars at the current rate. Thirty years ago the young, honeymooning Sloans stayed in this same hotel and paid the grand sum of twelve dollars. "Which included breakfast," says Meg, who, with her merciless memory for the cost of things, equivocates and subtracts and mildly despairs. Admittedly, though, there have been a number of improvements since that time: chiefly, tiny module bathrooms fitted into the corners of each room, and orange juice of an oddly dark hue served along with the croissants and coffee.

For ten days now they've sat at the same little table in the hotel breakfast room and buttered their already buttery croissants and helped themselves to apricot jam. Away from home, Meg abandons her dieting and exercise program. She grows careless and easy about her body which, in a matter of days, takes on a sleek, milky look. She has a different fragrance about her; her hands wander more rhythmically, almost musically.

Under Roy's knife the croissant shatters, leaving rings of tender flakes on the tablecloth, and one of these she picks up with the moistened tip of her finger and transfers to her tongue. Fresh flowers with tiny blue heads lean out of a glass bottle, an ordinary glass bottle, a vinegar bottle probably. Their waiter is young, square-jawed, from Holland. He's come to Paris to learn the business, he says, and also the French language, but to the Sloans he speaks a colloquial English, showing off. Clumsy but attentive, he brings a second jug of coffee without being asked, and more hot milk. Meg observes all this with a look of deep satisfaction; she tells Roy how rested and healthy she feels; already it seems she's forgotten she is the mother of a troubled daughter and the grandmother of two wearingly energetic children. Daylight enters the room in blocks and composes tall trembly shapes on the wallpaper behind her head. She is still a pretty woman. Roy wonders how long such prettiness lasts; his feeling is that any day now there will be an abrupt diminishment, and already he has begun to prepare himself for the tasks of pity and persuasion.

Before them, opened up on the table, is the map of Paris. They push the flowers to one side in order to make room, and Meg, with her reading glasses worn low on her nose, is pointing to the little red dot that is the Cluny Museum. Roy nods, takes a pen from his breast pocket and circles the dot. After a while they rise, sigh with contentment, and go into the street, stepping carefully around fresh dog turds, plentiful and perfectly formed, lying everywhere on the roughened oily pavement. They head for the Métro which is just around the corner.

Arm in arm they swing along. They feel younger in this foreign city, years younger than they do at home. The first few days in Paris were hectic and wasteful, but now everything has settled into a routine, and the two of them descend into the Métro with springy nonchalance, and blithely negotiate the turnstiles. After their first day they'd decided to buy a monthly pass, a *carte orange*, that bears their signature and photograph, and this document, more than anything else, carries them over an invisible frontier and makes them part of the wave of frowning commuters who flow through the gates and take possession of the platform. The Sloans have even acquired something of the Paris look of indifference and suffering, elbows tucked close to the body, feet sturdily planted, eyes directed inward as though recalling past holidays or rehearsing those to come: Brittany, the Alps, the spicy smell of forests, distances and vistas, here and yet not here, the Gallic knack of being everywhere and nowhere, of possessing everything and nothing.

At the entrance to the museum Roy counts out the exact change, thirty-two francs, and Meg opens her handbag automatically for inspection. Today there is the additional precaution of a body search. Smiling, they hold their arms straight out. A young man, who might be a student, frisks Roy by running his hands up and down his sides and between his legs; a broad-faced woman, biting her lips, performs the same swift operation on Meg.

The Sloans have been told that the bombs currently detonated in Paris are the size of three cigarette packets, and they naturally wonder what possible good these cursory inspections can do. They've concluded that the searches are symbolic, evidence that strict security measures are being observed, even though the situation is clearly impossible. Every day for a week now a bombing has occurred in Paris; yesterday the Hotel de Ville, the day before a suburban cafeteria. Armed soldiers, looking absurdly young and pitifully barbered, stand guard on street corners, but there *is* no cure, there *are* no effective measures. The attacks are too random and insidious. The city is too large.

And yet the Sloans show no signs of alarm. They

look relaxed and happy and, like everyone else entering the Cluny Museum this morning, they comply willingly when searched, even smiling at their inquisitors, anxious to demonstrate their innocence, their gratitude for care taken, their concern about the mounting gravity of the crisis, their feeling that, all things considered, America could easily be in a similar plight.

Once inside, arriving at the first of a series of exhibition rooms, they go their separate ways. They do this wordlessly, out of long habit. On the whole they have avoided the dismal symmetry of so many married couples. They confess their differences; they are people who move at different speeds. Their senses are differently angled. Meg's response to works of art is visual or tactile, Roy's is literal. Compulsively he studies titles and dates–stooping, squinting at the tiny print, drawing on his shaky Berlitz French to translate the brief explanations. Meg, on the other hand, stands well back with one hand cupping her chin, looking intently, absorbing and stowing away in some back compartment of her brain various shapes and colors and evolving patterns. She loves texture; she loves curious hand-wrought things; it doesn't matter to her if a tapestry–and the Cluny Museum is filled with tapestries–is six hundred years old or two hundred years. She looks for emblems and symbols and whimsical objects concealed in the muted backgrounds or receding borders, a fish motif, for example, or a mermaid or a lacework construction holding fruit. Whenever some detail strikes her forcefully, she rummages in her handbag for her pen and makes a notation, usually in the form of a little sketch.

Coming together afterward and discussing what they've seen, it's as though the Sloans have attended two separate exhibitions. Today they sit at a small round table in a bistro recommended by one of their many guidebooks, eating a light lunch, a salad of potatoes, watercress and walnuts. The pleasure of travel, Roy thinks, concentrates at these small public tables, he and Meg across from each other, composed for talk as they seldom are at home.

She can be an exasperating companion, nervous in the manner of pretty women, hovering, going off on tangents, sometimes given to finding untruthful reasons for the things she does, but, for all this, he prizes their intimacies. Away from home the boundaries between them loosen. He feels he can say anything, no matter how rambling or speculative, and be understood. She listens and nods. The shine in her eyes flatters him, and he is not, as he sometimes feels at home, a marauder in her busy, bracingly cluttered life. Now, today, she lifts her hands expressively, reversing her wrists, making an airy accompaniment for herself or perhaps for Roy or for the waiter in his floor-length apron. She is describing a particular gilded Virgin she saw this morning at the Cluny Museum. "At the Cluny," she says, innocently breezy, and Roy hears a swarm of echoes: *on the Champs, at the Luxembourg.* How soon his wife is able to slide her tongue around novelty, adopting what comes her way, without hesitation.

"What Virgin?" he asks.

"In that room, you know, that little anteroom where all the coins were."

"I didn't see any coins."

"They were in the same room. At least, I think it was the same room."

"I must have missed it completely."

"It was near the end," she tells him. "You were probably getting saturated, going in circles. I certainly was."

"I suppose I could go back this afternoon." Roy says this doubtfully at first.

"I loved her," says Meg, returning to the Virgin. "I *loved* her. Not that she was beautiful, she was more odd than beautiful. Her face, I mean. It was sort of frozen and pious, and she had these young eyes."

"How young?"

"Very. Like a teenager's eyes. They bulged. But the main thing was her stomach. Or her chest rather. It opened up, two little golden doors on hinges, beautiful, and inside was this tiny shelf. It was amazing, like a toy cupboard."

"And?"

"Inside her body, on this shelf–now this is pretty strange–was a whole crucifixion scene, all carved with little figures, tiny little things like dolls. I'm not describing it very well, but–"

He waits. He can smell her perfume across the table and is reminded of the measure of passion still stored at the heart of his feeling for her. He has given her this particular perfume, the same bottle every birthday. The buying of it, standing at a counter in a department store in Milwaukee and counting out bills, never fails to fill him with the skewed pleasure of the provider. An unwholesome pleasure nowadays, he has no doubt; dishonorable, his daughter Jenny would say, and something he should long ago have renounced.

"That's all," Meg says. "There she was, this little golden teenager, and inside her she was carrying a scene from the future. Like a video or a time bomb or something. It's the one thing I'll remember out of all that stuff we saw this morning. Just her." She presses a hand to her chest, her neat, buttoned suit jacket. "Opening up like that. It was–what will you remember?"

The question takes him by surprise. She means to surprise him, he's sure of it.

"The tapestries," he says finally.

"Which one?" She eyes him closely.

He is a little drunk; too little food with too much wine. Which one? He tries to focus, to think, then gives a helpless lopsided shrug. But Meg is poking in her bag for her address book, too preoccupied now to notice how aptly the gesture reflects his condition.

"Which one?"

"All of them," he says.

After lunch Meg leaves Roy sitting in the bistro.

Her best and oldest friend, Karen Craddock, has given her the address of a warehouse in north Paris where wonderful clothes can be had for a fraction of their retail cost. They are samples, according to Karen, worn once or twice by models in fashion shows, most of them in an American size eight, which is Meg's size–how she cherishes her smallness!–and also her daughter Jenny's.

Roy, whose feet ache, sits for an hour at the little table and makes himself drink two cups of bitter coffee. He reads the *Herald Tribune* carefully, item by item, concentrating, hoping to dispel the chalky pressure behind his eyes. Then he pays, puts on his damp raincoat and retraces his steps, back to the courtyard of the Cluny Museum.

Again he counts out money for a ticket, sixteen francs, wondering if the woman selling tickets is surprised to see him back so soon, such a zealous museum goer, so admirably greedy for an afternoon of art. She is as young as Jenny, with hair combed back roughly and a look on her face of scornful preoccupation. Stacking coins, arranging them in rows, she scarcely looks up. But the inspector, the amiable young guard who searched him earlier in the day, seems to remember him and, with a nod, waves him through.

Along with a light, early afternoon crowd, Roy enters the series of exhibition rooms. There are a great many of them, and they open logically, harmoniously, one into the next, but there are also odd turning points, raised or lowered levels and narrow staircases, a number of which are temporarily closed because of an ambitious archeological excavation going on beneath the building.

He has never had a sense of direction; it is an old family joke, how quickly he becomes lost. Within minutes today he is disoriented, twice returning to an odd, airy room holding the puzzling stone torsos of old kings and saints. He wonders if he should ask for assistance and tries to assemble a reasonable sentence. *Je cherche une vierge avec des portes sur sa poitrine.* Or is it *son poitrine*? Either way it sounds like the request of a madman.

And then, turning a corner, he finds her. She is

standing on a rough stone plinth in a corner of a little room behind a glass case of coins, somewhat smaller than he imagined from Meg's description, but yes, the eyes did bulge noticeably, looking heavenward, as though dully unaware of her bright golden belly, her unimaginable destiny. The two gilded doors stand open–Roy imagines they are perpetually open, locked at a forty-five degree angle, summoning the visitor's eye. And inside, like a scene from an old play, the tiny sorrow-bent figures enact their story.

He is not alone. An elderly man and woman, each with copious white hair and each leaning upon a wooden cane, pause, peer inside, and exchange creaky looks of amusement. Close behind them glowers a lean, unpretty woman in a leather coat that she has tried to brighten with a green scarf. She shakes her head and clicks her tongue sharply, perhaps with disapproval, perhaps with wonder–Roy is unable to tell. A moment later he hears the surprise of a deep American voice uttering the words ". . . distortion of time." Someone else, another man, replies with the speed of a ping-pong player, and also the frivolity. "Yes, of course, it does have a primitive feel, but it's actually quite a sophisticated rendering."

Roy steps back so the two men can have a clear view. Both are young, a tall, bony, raincoated pair. One carries a museum guide and regards the Virgin with hard critical eyes; the other has a priestly face and an expression of reverence. They are brothers, Roy thinks (that bony replication) or else, more probably, lovers. He longs to join in their discussion, if only to claim a bond with them, his fellow travelers. The feeling of belonging to a stalwart, foolhardy minority in an alien land gives Roy at times an unearned sense of the heroic which he recognizes as absurd. "What do you mean by 'primitive feel'?" he would like to ask, exaggerating his own midwestern vowels, but the two men move off–they seem to glide–leaving him alone with the Virgin.

He sees that her skin beneath the gold is smoothed wood, and her general outlines are stylized and conventional. She is really an ingenious little casket for the improbable sacrifice she bears, but her upward stare now strikes Roy as being impassively self-aware; certain covert bargains made in the past must now be paid for, and this payment, luridly dramatic, is rehearsed behind the pair of peek-a-boo doors. The silliness of art. The crude approximations. But he is moved, nevertheless, at the way a human life drains toward one revealing scene.

The doors themselves tempt him, especially their neatly worked hinges–but to touch them, he reasons, would probably set off an alarm. The whole museum is sure to be electronically monitored; it would be madness not to, given the current situation. He wonders if Meg had been similarly tempted, and thinks how she is always stopping to shut a bureau drawer, straighten a picture, adjust a chair cushion. She is more than just nervously neat; for Meg the believable world consists of touchable objects, mainly texture and angle and curve, that tremble above and powerfully rule her place in it. Or so he thinks, never having been able, even after all these years, to uncover her separate design or the source of her will.

He looks about and sees no one, though the density of the room seems to have shifted. He senses some material displacement, and at a distance hears what he believes to be the patter of rain falling on the ancient roof, a small fretful slap-slapping against stone. Quickly he reaches out and pushes one of the little doors. The tremor in his hand conveys itself to the mechanism, and it moves obediently in a small silken arc that delights him. But as he pushes it back to its original position he glimpses, at the periphery of his vision, a uniformed guard approaching.

The guard is wrinkled and stout with a squashed plum for a nose. The way he tilts his stoutness at Roy gives the impression of a formal, respectful bow, but his face is crimson–with anger, Roy thinks at first–and he speaks in a loud, throaty incomprehensible French and gestures roughly toward the entrance of the room.

Roy, in turn, points to the Virgin. He smiles benignly; he wants to protest that he's done no damage, only indulged a whim. *"Elle est si belle,"* he tries, anxious to placate the reddened face and show himself properly appreciative.

"You must leave the museum," the guard announces loudly.

Roy, amazed to hear a complete English sentence coming out of this cracked old face, defends himself. "I only touched the door," he protests. Then, "I'm very sorry."

"You must leave the museum." Louder this time.

To himself Roy says: This is ridiculous. He can hardly suppress a laugh. Here he is being scolded, reproved, being thrown out of a venerable French museum as if he were a teenage hooligan. He feels his arm firmly taken at the elbow. The old man's English apparently consists of a single phrase: "You must leave the museum."

Bewildered, Roy looks about, and then suddenly

understands. *Everyone* is being asked to leave the museum. The sound that a moment ago he had taken for rain was the sound of footsteps moving across the stone floors, of people rapidly leaving the exhibition rooms and heading for the main door. To the stout old guard who is already moving away from him, he mumbles a feeble chant–*merci, merci, merci.*

There are fifty, sixty people, maybe more, working their way to the entrance–where had they come from? Moments ago Roy had looked around and seen only a handful.

He is struck at first by how orderly the crowd is and how silently it moves along. Not one person is screaming or shouting–no one, in fact, is even talking–and how similar, too, they all seem in their breathy, melancholy, measured strides, hurrying through the calm rectangular rooms of crusted statuary and large loaf-shaped tombs; the tapestries, the porcelain, the examples of medieval glass, the paintings on wood. There is only a rattling, insectlike sound of clothing rubbing, swishing, long purposeful strides moving in waves, in a single direction.

And then something happens: for no discernible reason the gait changes. As though a signal has been given–but there has been no signal–everyone is running, and Roy too is running, squeezing through the narrow arches that divide the rooms, swerving, stumbling on his thick-soled shoes. Even the white-haired, cane-bearing couple seen earlier has somehow, by awkward shifts of weight and sideways lurching, contrived to run. A fat young woman with wild hair, a child under her arm, its head bobbing crazily, runs past Roy, and out of her frilled lips comes a wordless bleat of panic, an oink like a pig's squeal. And then the two bony American men brush past, one of them knocking against him and breathing a dutiful, constricted *pardon.*

The overhead lights blink several times. Coins jingle in Roy's pocket. As he runs toward the exit he is thinking of nothing. Or rather, he thinks about how he is thinking of nothing. The cemented accumulation, all he has banked away inside his head, seems suddenly vaporized and lifted; everything outside the minute, *this* minute, falls away, the idle stories that pass through his brain late at night, the alternative choices he might have made, his lazy indifference and absurd fumblings. Newspapers, books, shifts of allegiance. Minor cruelties, a teacher who once said of an essay he'd written, "Where hath grammar flown." Meg emerging from the house one winter day, fastening her coat. Inca sculpture and lost phone numbers; a brief flirtation with a very young woman, how it came to nothing; snowbanks; trees; Jenny returning early from camp with a rash on her back; Jenny bringing Kenneth home for the first time and saying with light irony, "Meet Mr. Perfect." A platter holding an immense turkey, heartless strategies, unremitting dialogue, the names of certain wild flowers, even the minor present pain of arthritis in his left thumb, a thumb broken at the age of eight, bent backwards on the asphalt schoolyard by someone whose name has just this minute slipped away. It has all slipped away. Nothing, not even the smallest spindle of thought, impedes his progress as he runs through room after room toward the main door of the Cluny Museum.

He stumbles at last through the foyer and sees, dreamily, that the ticket booth has been abandoned, the insolent girl vanished. Then he is in the cobbled courtyard, and then the street beyond. There he sees a number of paneled trucks, their windows lowered, the dark squares starred with the faces of boylike soldiers, numbly staring back at him. A few soldiers stand on the pavement, clustered around the main door, and it maddens Roy to see how one of them lolls, *lolls*, against the wall. "What happened?" he asks, but already he knows. Nothing has happened, only a false alarm.

One of the young American men is vomiting quietly into a tub of begonias, and the other, he of the sacerdotal face, is standing by and murmuring, *Jesus, Jesus*. The fat girl with wild hair comes over to Roy and tells him she is from New York, Long Island. Roy explains he is from Milwaukee. The stringent circumstances make their brief exchange feel dreamlike and discordant. The white-haired couple explain they are from California. Their serious leathery faces suggest the pathos of good intentions and an unslaked hunger for human contact. They have been coming to France for twenty years, they tell Roy, and have never seen anything like this.

He walks back to the hotel, telling himself that the fresh air will do him good and, in fact, the rhythm of his shoes on the cement does bring calm–a man in a boy's shoes–as does the sight, a mere two streets away, of people selling melons and entering cafés. A well-brushed dog dances on a leash; its owner dances along behind. Every face Roy sees is clothed with the dumb shine of ignorance. He wonders, already he wonders, how he will describe this scene to Meg; he remembers nothing but the old guard tipping his capacious belly toward him and saying, "You must leave the museum." And how he ran stumbling out of the museum door into the courtyard. He is emptied out, light-headed, agonizingly alert. He feels he's been as close to the edge of his life as he's ever likely to be.

Meg and Roy Sloan will not always be sitting here at a little square table in La Petite Fourchette dining on marinated crab, roasted lamb cutlets with green beans, followed by a selection of cheeses, followed by sorbet cassis, followed by coffee and by two glasses of brilliantly colored cognac. The authentic world will sweep them away, attributing their brief incandescence to the lamplight or the shift of weather or the conjoined sense of having escaped what they didn't even know they dreaded.

"Of course you ran," pretty Meg Sloan says to her husband. "Anyone would run. There's nothing shameful about wanting to save your own life. I mean, there's nothing selfish about it or cowardly. If the house were on fire, you'd run out of it, wouldn't you? I know I would. I'd run like crazy."

Her shopping expedition to north Paris has failed. The warehouse, when she finally found it, had been filled with tourists much like herself, women of about her own age and size and possessed of the same financial ease and concentrated fervor. These women carried, too, the accumulated heft of discouragement; the clothes offered for sale were ugly and soiled and brought to mind instances of similar discouragement. Meg tried on one two-hundred-dollar dress that transformed her into an aged dwarf and brought tears to her eyes.

Her diminutive size, her chief vanity, seemed all at once shameful, contrived and unwholesome. She fled to a nearby post office and placed a long-distance call to her daughter in Milwaukee. The call went through quickly, much to her surprise, and caught Jenny in the throes of packing–she had patched things up with Kenneth; an understanding had been reached, a compromise of sorts, and she and the children were about to return to Green Bay. The weather in Wisconsin was glorious, frost at night, but temperatures in the daytime that qualified as Indian summer. The shrubs in the front yard had just started to turn.

Hanging up the telephone, still thrumming with her daughter's voice, its dying vibrancy, Meg had felt divided and dizzy, as though she had stepped into a room where the air was thinned and, at the same time, more tremblingly present. She was afraid she might faint or else choke and, for that reason, took a taxi back to the hotel.

"It was total extravagance," she tells Roy. "When I had my *carte orange* right in my purse. And phoning in the middle of the afternoon like that, at the most expensive time. On an impulse. I just felt–"

"It was money well spent," Roy assures her, knowing he will forever, in one way or another, be called upon for reassurance.

"We talked for ages," Meg then confesses. "I could have bought that hideous dress for the same price."

"Years from now," he tells her, "you'll look back and you'll never count the cost. You won't even remember it."

The Sloans recognize but resist the details of the future, just as Meg knows about but can't see the friable skin of her breasts beneath her white sweater, and Roy the bald, highly burnished spot on the back of his head. They will get older, of course. One of them will die first–the world will allow this to happen–and the other will live on for a time. Their robust North American belief that life consists of stages keeps them from sinking, though ahead of them, in a space the size of this small table, waits a series of intricate compromises: impotence, rusted garden furniture, disordered dreams, and the remembrance of specific events which have been worn smooth and treacherous as the stone steps of ancient buildings. A certain amount of shadowy pathos will accrue between what they remember and what they imagine, and eventually one of them, perhaps lying limply on a tautly made-up bed, will gruesomely sentimentalize this Paris night. The memory will divide and shrink like a bodily protein, and terror, with all its freshness and redemptive power, will give way, easily, easily, to the small rosy singularity of this shaded lamp, and the arc of light that cuts their faces precisely in half.

Block Out

The writer Meershank, vacationing in Portugal with his wife-cum-editor, Maybelle Spritz, became blocked.

The two of them spent their first morning there exploring the coastal city of Porto, which is an airy gemlike city that, as Maybelle complained, had been severely underrated–given one lousy star in the *Michelin Guide*, that was all. This was plain crazy, a single star for a dozen broad sun-splashed terraces, for countless baroque churches, for the elegant iron bridges, and the lazy smoky river lined with pungent fishing boats and dark bars. Ridiculous! She was indignant. She slapped the green guide book hard against her long thigh. Coming to Portugal had been her idea. She was the one who had thought of flight, of leaving the Ontario winter behind, who had persuaded and cajoled and weakened her husband Meershank, and she was determined to unearth treasures for him hour by hour. Now this insult, this chintzy rating, a gorgeous city awarded one grudging star.

"And just listen," Maybelle said to Meershank, stopping in the middle of a steep, winding cobbled street to consult the despised guide. "We're supposed to 'note the gaily colored laundry flapping overhead'. Laundry! I ask you. Never mind this incredible architecture all around us, we're asked to gape at mended tablecloths and old underpants."

Meershank looked upward. Was it the word underpants that caught his attention? Or Maybelle's brightly injured North American scorn, her admirable readiness to admire, and to deplore the kingly judgments of rubber tire merchants. So what does this uncultivated bunch know from anything? Back in Canada, she told Meershank, the least of these little Portuguese churches would have caused a major fussing over. A plastic dome built to protect the gold leaf and blue tiles. Tickets sold, conducted tours given, voices hushed toward a proper reverence. But here amid the riches of Portugal, tourists were asked to gaze at laundry! The condescension, the perversity! And what did the owners of the laundry have to say about it? Were they consulted about their contribution to the city's ambience? Adjured in the name of folklore to keep their colorful laundry flying? Don't you bet your sweet heart on it.

Socks, sheets, aprons, brassieres. Meershank took them in, groping for a portion of his wife's contempt. He respected cleanliness, that was the problem. He liked the thought of clothes whipped by soapy water and then bright air. Work pants, blankets–and were those diapers? Ah, diapers, yes, half a dozen in a neat row, holding hands as it were. Seeing them he felt, finally, a throat swell–wah!–of delectable sentiment.

That was the moment when his foot slipped. He felt his leg joint pull brutally at its moorings, and for a second he struggled grotesquely for balance, but to no effect. Then he was spread on the stone street, a man of some sixty-five years, lying on his back, his four limbs pointed in four different global directions.

There he rested, as grounded as any being can get, a cartoon splat: Meershank Sprawled.

A prolific and successful writer of comic novels, he immediately thrust about for droll possibilities. None appeared. He knew only that the separate points of his pain were cleanly pinned down: back-of-head, left buttock, right elbow, and a hand that was skinned and already oozing.

Around him gathered a circle of curious, amiable faces, grave but unalarmed. They drew closer. And coming into focus was his wife Maybelle, squatting at his side. She wore long dangling earrings faced with mirrors, and white Bermuda shorts rucked back to reveal knees and thighs like waxed maple. She was crooning, or should he say keening? He loved her dearly, but had not perceived until now that she was a keening woman. Aieee! On and on; he thought the moment beautiful.

Then he saw *it*. Turning his head a quarter of an inch away from Maybelle's polished knees, he glimpsed the object that had brought him down, the agent of his disgrace. *It* was a piece of common street rubbish, a blackened, stinking, fly-encircled scrap of vegetable matter–a banana peel no less.

Here was something he hadn't known he feared: the outrageous collision of reality and art, but art in its putrefied form. Even in his earliest novels, those puerile works he no longer bothered to list in *Who's Who* (*Babylon Babydoll*, *Schlepping Right Along*) he had never fallen so low as to employ a banana peel. True, in his extravagant farce *School for Sandals* about corruption in the shoemakers' academy, he had brought the class bully, Jack Boot, down on the playing field with a slice of rotted baloney. But baloney was not bananas. There were limits. The lowest comedy has its first plateau morality.

"Do you think you can stand up?" Maybelle was saying into his ear. "Have you broken anything?"

"Just my spirit," Meershank actually said, and winced with shame.

Further south, in the city of Lisbon, there were more churches to visit. Meershank lost count, but Maybelle made special claims for every last one. "Gorgeous," she said again and again, adding her expelled awe to the jumble of gilded relics and saints' gizzards. In shallow stone niches were dozens of sullen virgins with swords thrust into their chests. "Our Lady of Sorrows," Maybelle read from her *Michelin Guide.* Seven swords for the seven sorrows.

Our Lady?–Meershank's bone marrow liquefied. He is willing enough when required to lower his Hebraic antenna for the sake of art, but rebels at that tetchy pronoun *our*. And the designation *lady* with its suggestion of parasol and gloves. And only seven sorrows? Was that all? Such a nice finite number. She should relax, take it easy. Why this grimacing forbearance? It was embarrassing.

The bruise on his left hip had grown increasingly painful and, standing in the backs of chilly churches, one blue and golden marvel after another, he felt himself going stiff. Maybelle at last looked his way and guessed. "You're exhausted," she said. "We've earned ourselves a good lunch," and hauled him off to a large clean expensive restaurant where English was spoken and where they were served cold white wine and grilled sardines so tender and crisp that even the tiny tails begged to be picked up and eaten. Meershank at that instant felt he understood the point of gluttony. Eating, drinking, spreading, appreciating, he entertained a vision of an afternoon nap back at the hotel. A siesta; what could be more appropriate? He smiled across at Maybelle who smiled back. Smooth sheets waiting to be mussed.

"Now," Maybelle said, not so easily deterred, "for the *pièce de résistance.*"

They took a taxi to the Museum of Ancient Art, hurried past dark oily paintings of the Annunciation, of St. Anthony being tempted and retempted, portraits of sly, chinless burghers and archbishops and several more sword-struck virgins. "Almost there," Maybelle said, pointing, leading Meershank around a corner.

Ah!–there it stood! *The Adoration of St. Vincent.* A howling wall of color. Maybelle, satisfied to have found what she was after, consulted her book. "Thank God! Three stars! At last a little respect."

The six looming panels showed the saints of Portugal in all their homely wide-staring good nature. Meershank, who loved crowds, who respected healthy conviviality, felt instant affection for this mob. Besides saints there were peering, squinting beggars, knights, princes, fishermen, Queen Isabella herself, and a single Jew–all of history's gaudy gang jamming together at an impromptu hour. There was nothing here that could be deconstructed. The faces, the postures, the cheerful way they overlapped and huddled and made human space for each other suggested folks out for a picnic. And the eyes, so strong, serious and clever; the eyes were something else; in the eyes Meershank read a mission to remap the world of good and evil.

Maybelle, lost in her book, whispered something in Meershank's ear.

He croaked back. "Eh?"

"Nuno Gonsalves," she repeated, looking up.

"What's that?"–reverting to the role of curmudgeon abroad.

"The painter. That's his name. Nuno Gonsalves. Fifteenth century." Maybelle was going whispery again. "One of the treasures of Portugal."

"I see." One of the treasures. (That fragrant word.)

"Well, what do you think?" Maybelle hissed. "Pretty damn magnificent, isn't it?"

Meershank's tongue sought a sprig of irony. A pun to stick between his teeth, or a sharp little anachronism, finely sprung, needle-bright. This whispery place needed a dose of irreverence, a dollop of protein, but what?

"Yes," he said to the startled Maybelle, forsaking

all verbal horseplay and looking upward. The silver
of a tear glinted, and with a straight face he said,
"Magnificent."

Prolific Meershank. Fecund and procreative
Meershank, fructifying and endlessly flowering. The
cornucopia of his imagination spills and pours its
lazy plenitude, reseeding itself annually. A book a
year, sometimes two. Milch-cowishly he brings them
forth–this has been going on for three decades now.
The man needs a stopper for his brain. Who said
that? Who? One of his jealous contemporaries
probably, who else? What a one Meershank is to
weave, forge, chisel, carve, invent, turn upside down.
His fictions come off the high dive. They shoot the
rapids. They burble up out of deep sleep. *Doesn't
that man ever rest?* (Again the jaundiced rival,
gemmed with malice.)

Of course Meershank worries about his fertility,
what fool wouldn't? In his famous parodic novel,
Leapfrog Lottery, didn't the aging protagonist, also a
writer, also a family man, beg for mercy, ask to be
manacled, demand a lobotomy and, when all else
failed, conspired in the kidnapping and murder of
his own word processor? (But true peace came only
in the final chapter when a prestigious writing
award brought on a case of instant and permanent
paralysis.)

Meershank has never been able to understand the
devils that drive him to extravagance, since in his
private life he is a man of moderation. He lives in an

unpretentious three-bedroom house at Jacksons Point, Ontario. He has exactly two children, well-behaved intelligent daughters, now grown-up. He has had two wives only, and loved them both; his first marriage of thirty-five years ended with his wife's death, and his second to his editor, Maybelle Spritz, is now in its third year. Maybelle is younger than Meershank, in her early forties, attractive and slender, but hardly in a class with Cécé Valentine. (Cécé, girl-tramp of Meershank's novel *Continuous Purring*, is considered his most Lolita-like creation, abundantly sexed, immoderately luscious, with verbiage fluttering from her lips in a blizzard of concupiscence.) No, Maybelle's wifely moderation matches the Meershank mode, as steadfast and contained as Meershank himself.

So why this writerly excess? Meershank knows immortality lies in a single quatrain, a couplet even, which is why, when he looks at the double shelves of his published books—not including paperbacks or translations—he thinks: silage, ashes. He's been ready for years to cut back, but doesn't know how. What would he do with his expendable time? He wakes in the morning with a headful of chat. It feels like a sinus infection coming on, a mosquito army. The pressure is terrible. He doesn't, has never had, the inclination to relieve the pain with alcohol or tennis. Also out of the question are gardening, long walks, birdwatching, going to the movies, going anywhere in fact. It took Maybelle feats of timing and melodrama to get him to Portugal. She caught him off guard, between books, and held out the only sure-fire temptation she knew: the promise of material. Portugal could be mined. Gawking tourists could be made to wriggle and squeal. The awful little fates and embarrassments of dislocation could be polished up for chortles, ground down fine for guffaws and snorts, made waxy and pointed with winks and nudges. Well, yes.

But then came the humiliation of the Porto banana peel, and a week later the painting of Nuno Gonsalves, Portugal's treasure.

Meershank, moved by the astonishing work of art, asked Maybelle to show him some more of the artist's work. He snapped his fingers like a tap dancer; might as well take in the lot while he was in town.

"That's it," Maybelle said, stowing the guide book in her woven bag.

"That's what?"

"*It.* All there is."

"You're kidding. You mean the man painted one picture and quit?'

"As far as anyone knows. That's what's so miraculous. He did it once and he did it right."

His heart winced. Dear cruel Maybelle. She couldn't know how the words stung. Meershank would have sulked if he hadn't been so tired. His feet were tired, his head was tired. He was tired of art, tired of travel, tired of the big golden sun shining on his bare head. Enough already. One more week and he could go home.

His brain especially was in bad shape, stuffed up with sadness and red dust. Waking early in strange hotels he found himself running a cheering video through his head: his own bed back home, Maybelle in the kitchen aggressively juicing a pair of oranges, the view from their back window down the long snow-covered slope of yard, the furnace doing its sweet business day in and day out.

The high-tech quality of his reveries made him ashamed but happy, especially the flicker of his own surprising image, for there he was in his old red cardigan, still at the kitchen window, indolent, sipping cold coffee to damp down the dust, staring happily at a rectangle of sky. His desk and his word processor, it seemed, had vanished. There was nothing there but a poor old idle duffer–himself–smiling.

On their second-to-last day in Portugal, Meershank and Maybelle came across something odd. This was in the old city of Braga, in the famous cathedral. There, on the altar of one of the side chapels, they saw dozens of human parts molded in wax. "They're called *ex votos*," whispered Maybelle, quoting from the merciless guide book. "They're sort of like concrete prayers, you might say."

Among the clutter Meershank saw wax legs, wax ears, wax hands, wax breasts, kidneys and hearts. Presumably these pale yellow bodily facsimiles had been placed at the feet of the Virgin in the hope of invoking miraculous healing. Some of them were gray with dust and fly dirt and looked as though they had lain there for years. Meershank stood well back. He found something hideous, but also innocent about their naked abandonment. He stared, then touched. The deposition, stiffened and discolored, had nothing left of original pleading, but only a candid, almost careless resignation. He found himself wanting to dive into that carelessness, to merge with it. To throw up his hands in the old classic gesture of defeat, open-palmed: so be it.

The next day, leaving Portugal, stepping with Maybelle aboard the Boeing 747 and allowing himself to be strapped in by a strapping air hostess, Meershank felt, happily, that he too had left something behind; his hands lay majestic and idle on his lap. Then the bulk of his body rose in the air, carrying with it its new lightness and sudden tight band of silence.

He loved his writer's block. Back home he found that the affliction fit him perfectly, the way a chestful of air fills a baritone's lungs. This was a silence that could be settled into. Some of life's essence stirred in it. He embraced it wholly, though for Maybelle's sake he put on a stricken face, especially in the mornings, meeting her agitated concern over the coffee pot.

"Have a second cup," Maybelle cried. "Have a third." Buoyancy was what she tried for on these mornings. Her large handsome bony face composed itself into vital lines, wifely empowerment. She was learning how to put on a good show of bustle. She trilled and sang. She exhorted, at first subtly, then openly. The day was ready to be packed with accomplishment; the morning hours especially squeaked their need. "More toast," she warbled. "Try this high fiber stuff, today just may be the day." She passed butter, jam, honey, seeing in the melting calories the fuel for creation. On the way out the door, all shine and forward motion, she beamed back a smile. "A breakthrough's on the way. I feel it in my bones."

Three days a week she drove off to Toronto where she worked for a large publishing house. All spring

she'd been toiling over several manuscripts simultaneously, one of them a thousand pages long. This
particular extravaganza she was trimming down to
size, but it grieved her to throw words in a wastebas-
ket when at home they were in short supply, had
dried up completely, in fact; six months since she and
Meershank had returned from Portugal and not a
single paragraph written. "Anything?" she would ask
briskly, coming home at the end of the working day.
Meershank might be reading the paper on the side
veranda or brushing down the dog or clipping a
hedge.

"Nothing today." His voice was cheerful. Ordinary.
Life going on.

"How about trading up to a new word processor?"
Maybelle suggested, a fishy shine on her face. "That
monster of yours is positively antiquated."

Another day, she sprang more wildly. "Have you
ever thought of a pen?" she said. "Remember
pens?"

Workmen arrived one morning and installed a new
skylight in his study. "Surprise!" Maybelle said. "An
early birthday present."

Accustomed to Meershank's activity, she found its
cessation worrying. She connected it with depression, and being a woman, particularly the woman she
was, she linked his depression with herself, some
failing on her part, some act omitted.

But Meershank was happy in his inactivity, he swore
it. He felt—what?—fond of himself, fonder than he
had for years, this pathetic stricken fellow caught in

the human tide. It was a relief after his long gilded hubris to be among the dispossessed, newly numbed before his art which was growing steadily more noble as it slipped out of his reach. So this was what it was like, this agony of drought. Hmmmmm. Well, now he knew. He felt curiously flattered to be one with his fellows, those sincere scribblers he had so avidly avoided and scorned. Fraternity renewed him, the communal part of himself–here he stood, witness to the feast and famine of the creative cycle. The suffering of the throttled was his, and he felt appropriately shriven, haunted, beset and blessed. Hadn't he always suspected that profligacy could be cured, austerity accomplished? A spare Beckettish brevity might yet come his way–he could at least hope–or failing that, well, silence. Why the hell not?

Filling time was not nearly the problem he had imagined since hours could be spent thinking about getting started, and further hours cursing the darkness, making false starts and reading them aloud with rich grunts of disgust. Crumpling sheets of paper was a satisfying activity and could be done very, very slowly. A whole hour–generally following a lunch of warmed-up soup–could be devoted to philosophical speculation, addressing that fleshy, many-fingered question: does the world really need another book? No. Yes. No. Well, it depended, didn't it? (One of the treasures of Portugal, one of the treasures of. . . .)

Or he could give himself over to gossip, to speculation. The publishing world being what it was, he imagined that word had got round: ungirdled, unbraked Meershank had been brought to heel.

(Serves the old boy right.) It was July. Then came August. His first bookless autumn was fast approaching. The thought was crisp, bracing. He inhaled it with a sense of awe. There were tragic proportions here if he cared to take them up, but why should he? One more wordsmith muzzled, the old babbler, the old conveyor belt, scribbler, stumbler. Arghhhh!

Idleness, and an impulse for self-flagellation, led him to the reading of book reviews. Just how were his fellow *écrivains* faring? Aha!–there was old S– with yet another of his prolix empty potherings; didn't the man realize his life's work was nothing but goosedown! Had he no respect for the value of words, the craft itself, its intrinsic gold?

These pious, envious pangs were delicious to Meershank; he couldn't get enough.

"It's my fault," Maybelle grieved, "for dragging you to Portugal."

"No," he told her truthfully, it had started before Portugal, almost a year before.

He had been invited to a Toronto TV station for what was to be an in-depth interview. He arrived promptly in the late afternoon and discovered that the interview slot had been double-booked. Would he mind, Nana Beanflower asked him, if she went ahead and interviewed Slas Stanley, the figure skater, first? "Not at all," said Meershank. He knew his adopted country, he knew his place in it. Besides, what was half an hour in a lifetime?

He had come to discuss, promote that is, his latest book, *Maple Foot Jelly*, and couldn't help noticing when his turn came that Ms Beanflower, a fresh copy in hand, had stuck her bookmark at what looked like page ten. An old story: too busy to read, these media youngsters. "Shall we begin?" she said violently.

Her hair was brilliant media orange and she wore violet clothing made of layers of wrinkled cotton. Her feet in their thong sandals could have been cleaner. Meershank took a keen interest in costume, believing it revealed what the north half of the brain repressed, but Ms Beanflower, he decided, seemed unsteady in her yearnings. Still, he had not come to analyze; he had come to discuss his new book.

The plot first. They always wanted the plot; they thought it mattered. Then a little personal background, what was he working on next, his thoughts about the dark side of humor, what he was really saying underneath all his puns and jabber.

"I really *am* saying what I'm saying," Meershank said wearily, slipping thinly away from her gaze.

"Ah, come on now?" The voice coy. The twinkle turned on high.

"There *are* no hidden meanings, Ms Beanflower."

She bit her lip wickedly, leaned close to the microphone and said, "They say you're an old toughie, Meershank, but do you know what you remind me of?"

"No, what?" he said stupidly.

"A great big teddy bear, that's what."

"Ah."

In the following weeks he speculated on what might have been a fitting reply to this announcement. Thank you? Pardon? This interview is now terminated? Would you tell John Updike or Slas Stanley or Pierre Trudeau that *he* looked like a teddy bear? What exactly does a teddy bear look like? Is looking like a teddy bear something that serious and enlightened men aspire to? Is it media policy to pin labels on the teddy bear minority? Is this resemblance to a teddy bear physical or metaphysical? Is a teddy bear man lovable or grotesque? Deeply cute or profoundly shameful?

It was a mistake, he knew, to take Nana Beanflower seriously. What lapped between her ears was orange Jello. What motivated her was the wish to be adorable. Nevertheless she had managed to make him doubt himself. Something intensely frivolous about his work, about himself, had encouraged her contempt, entered his body, and deeply injured him. A sword stuck in his chest.

And that, he told his wife Maybelle, skipping the details, had been the real start of his writer's block.

Maybelle Spritz knew what it was to be blocked.

As a young woman of twenty-five, starting work in a large publishing house, she had been appointed Meershank's editor. It was a fluke for someone so young to be assigned a major writer, but somebody or other in charge had had the wit to see that the Spritz warp matched the Meershank woof.

She loved him from the first day, falling upon his scrambled, pencil-whorled manuscripts, her hands flying over the stacked pages, smoothing them hot or cool, taking possession. Turning over the sheets she often laughed her big-girl laugh. Other times she circled and queried. It was said she had the Meershank canon by heart. But that was all she had.

Every year on her birthday he took her to lunch; Zuckerman's on Bathurst, boiled noodles and brisket. At Christmastime he bought her items that reflected the privacy of his affection, jokey jewelry or sternly ironic travel books, one year a beautiful seashell, another time a blue teapot shaped like a flower and covered with images of itself.

And she was always included at the Meershank's annual Boxing Day parties. There in the crowded scented noisy house, whose windows and banisters were trimmed with holly, Maybelle was embraced by Meershank's adored wife Louise, that good and gentle, blameless and bloomingly pretty woman.

These parties made Maybelle go dreamy. Always she drove out to Jacksons Point with the idea of taking a single cup of punch and slice of holiday cake, then fleeing. But year after year she was seduced, before she knew it snuggled between the cushions of a broad tufted sofa and told she was irreplaceable, priceless, one of the family, a fiction she fleetingly–that is, for an hour or so–believed.

This went on for fifteen years. She adored Meershank, not so much ardently as hopelessly, and sometimes she forgot about it for days at a time. A kind of lankiness came over her as she got older. She grew taller, it seemed, along with her name and title: Maybelle Spritz, Senior Editor. Her own office. A member of the Board. Meershank came more and more to rely on her judgment, and his twenty-ninth book, *Monkey Funk*, was dedicated to "The Spritziest Girl in Town." That made her bawl.

It never occurred to her, even in her dreams, that Meershank's wife would grow ill, would die, and that Meershank would be "free." (Maybelle Spritz is a clever woman with a blue pencil, a sorceress some say, but she lacks basic imagination.) Her life had taken a particular shape and could not be reinvented. It wasn't so terrible. She had her friends, her holidays, her work, her birthday lunches, her Boxing Day tributes. She wasn't crippled or crazy. She wasn't dead.

She was only blocked.

Maybelle brought her blocked husband smoked fish wrapped in butcher's paper. Also wonderful pears. Also gossip, sweet as candy. But the truth is, though it is very seldom admitted to, there is very little anyone can do for anyone else. Interesting excursions can be planned, people invited to dinner, noodle puddings produced, orange juice squeezed, lamps left burning, bed covers turned invitingly down. Kisses can be dropped on the tops of heads, and news brought from one person's world to another, but in the end it's a matter of waiting things out in an improvised shelter and thinking as kindly of yourself as possible.

Mimi Cornblossom (purple curls, orange garments) is the heroine show-biz star of Meershank's new book, published the third week in December, and bearing the generic title *Blockbuster*; it made this year's fall list by a split hair's breadth. A rollicking read, a hydra-headed offering, it has the same off-the-kitchen-wallishness as Meershank's pre-block books, and also a style that's teased and tenderized by all-night writing sessions, late-hour editing, and a dangerous drive to the printers over narrow, icy streets. It's a broth of old injuries and pleasures, of the wounded heart and its stitched-up hole. Actual writing time? A dozen November days; for Meershank a record.

The prologue has Mimi waking one morning with a tune in her head, a tune she can't place. It's a talky, sparky tune, full-lipped and bright. She carries it with her to The Narcissus Pool where she works as a manicurist, and all day long as she pushes back cuticles and trims and files and polishes she feels a set of lyrics beating at her temples, stabbing her through the stomach.

It's driving her crazy trying to figure out where this song comes from, its Latin sunniness and breezy flash. She hums and jerks, and breaks an emery board across the nail of an elderly client, forgets to eat lunch, jingles the coins in her uniform pocket, eyes the clock, stares out the window.

She asks everyone she sees about the song: her best friend Virgie Allgood, her fiancé Ken Kool, her little nephew Lester Lou. "That's a great tune," they all say, but no one knows where it comes from.

It skips into her dreams, waxy, amber, hollow. There's a forward lean on it now, and some unexpected punctures that by morning have been repaired. She smiles in the mirror, wincing at her own hot puzzled face. Two days ago her head was empty and now it's filled with a chorus and kickline. What is this?

She puts in a call to her favorite rock station and

does a version for Big Larry. "Wild," is what he says. Then, "Solid!" Then, "Hey, you got yourself a real high spinner there."

"I do?" she says. "Really?" And feels a small brass gear of consciousness engage. She's no fool: she's got a good voice, not a great voice, but this is her tune. *Hers*!

Between the old Mimi and the new Mimi lies the thinnest of membranes. It's made out of air. It's colorless. It's not in the dictionary, not in the phone book, not in the bureau drawers or hall cupboard, but does this worry Mimi Cornblossom?

Of course not. She's already slipped like a fish into Meershank's Chapter 1, and now she's rehearsing for Chapter 2. She's got treasure to unearth and plot lines to bind. Suffering waits for her, and recompense too. Ending and mending, squaring and cubing. There she goes, there she goes! Eyes wide open, lurching blindly into the future.

Collision

Today the sky is solid blue. It smacks the eye. A powerful tempered ceiling stretched across mountain ranges and glittering river systems: the Saône, the Rhine, the Danube, the Drina. This unimpaired blueness sharpens the edges of the tile-roofed apartment block where Martä Gjatä lives and hardens the wing tips of the little Swiss plane that carries Malcolm Brownstone to her side. What a dense, dumb, depthless blue it is, this blue; but continually widening out and softening like a magically reversed lake without a top or bottom or a trace of habitation or a thought of what its blueness is made of or what it's *for*.

But take another look. The washed clarity is deceiving, the yawning transparency is fake. What we observe belies the real nature of the earth's atmosphere which is adrift, today as any day, with biographical debris. It's everywhere, a thick swimmy blizzard of it, more ubiquitous by far than earthly salt or sand or humming electrons. Radio waves are routinely pelted by biography's mad static, as Martä Gjatä, trying to tune in the Vienna Symphony, knows only too well. And small aircraft, such as the one carrying Malcolm Brownstone eastward across Europe, occasionally fall into its sudden atmospheric pockets. The continents and oceans are engulfed. We are, to speak figuratively, as we more and more do, as we more and more *must* do, smothering in our own narrative litter-bag.

And it keeps piling up. Where else in this closed lonely system can our creaturely dust go but up there on top of the storied slag heap? The only law of biography is that everything, every particle, must be saved. The earth is alight with it, awash with it, scoured by it, made clumsy and burnished by its steady accretion. Biography is a thrifty housewife, it's an old miser. Martä Gjatä's first toddling steps are preserved and her first word–the word *sjaltë*, which means honey–and her dead father's coldly aimed praise–"For a girl you have sharp ways about you."

These are fragments, you say, cracker crumbs, lint in your shirt pocket, dizzy atoms. They're off the map, off the clock, floating free, spring pollen. That's the worst of it: there's nothing selective about biography's raw data, no sorting machine, no briny episodes underlined in yellow pencil or provided with bristling asterisks–it's all here, the sweepings and the leavings, the most trivial personal events encoded with history. Biography–it sniffs it out, snorts it up.

Here, to give an example, is Malcolm Brownstone's birth squawl from fifty-odd years ago, a triple-note *yawolll* of outrage bubbling up through the humid branches of his infant lungs, and again, *yawolll*. And the sleepless night he spent, aged twelve, in a rain-soaked tent in the Indian Hills, and also the intensity with which he reads newspapers and promptly forgets most of what he reads, and his dreamy neurotic trick of picking up a spoon and regarding his bent face in the long sad oval of its bowl.

In a future world, in a post-meltdown world, biography may get its hands on the kind of cunning conversion that couples mass and energy. We may learn, for instance, to heat our houses with it, build bigger lasers with its luminous run-off or more concentrated fictive devices.

But for the time being, every narrative scrap is equally honored and dishonored. Everything goes into the same democratic hopper, not excluding the privately performed acts of deceased spinners and weavers, or contemporary ashtray designers and manicurists, or former cubists and cabinet ministers, and young mothers pushing prams and poets who seek to disarm their critics–even these seemingly inconsequential acts enter the biographical aggregation and add to the weight of the universe.

It's crowded, *is it ever crowded*! Inside a single biographical unit, there are biographical clouds and biographical shadows, biographical pretexts and strategies and time-buying sophistries and hair-veined rootlets of frazzled memory. Long complex biographies, for example, have been registered and stored for all the ancestors, friends and acquaintances of the Japanese pop singer, who right this minute is strolling in the sunshine down the Champs Élysées wearing a leopard (genuine) jacket and a pair of pale pressed jeans. There are detailed dossiers for each of the twelve girls and twenty-six boys who competed for the state whistling championship in Indianapolis in 1937. Every particular is recorded, and also every possibility and random trajectory, even those, to cite the case of Martä G. and Malcolm B., that have only a partial or wishful existence.

Written biography, that's another matter, *quite* another matter! Memoirs, journals, diaries. Works of the bio-imagination are as biodegradable as orange peels. Out they go. Psssst–they blast themselves to vapor, cleaner and blonder than the steam from a spotless kettle. Nothing sticks but the impulse to get it down. Consider Martä Gjatä's four great-grandfathers. Three of them were illiterate shepherds; the fourth was a famous autodidact, a traveler, a minor politician, a poet of promise and, in his old age, the writer of a thick book entitled *The Story of My Life* (Lexoni Bardhë Këtë). Copies of this book can still be found in rural libraries throughout the Balkans, but not a word of the text has entered the cosmology of biography, of which the four great-grandfathers, shepherds and sage alike, have a more or less equal share.

Martä herself does not keep a diary, living as she does in a part of the world where one's private thoughts are best kept private. She is a droll, intelligent woman of wide-ranging imagination, as anyone on the streets of her city will tell you, but the one thing she cannot imagine is her encounter, just a few hours away, with the large, clean-faced, bald-headed North American named Malcolm Brownstone. The meeting, if such a slight wordless collision can be called a meeting, will originate in the lace-curtained coffee salon of the Hotel Turista. She will arrive early, a few minutes before Malcolm Brownstone, and will wear a green checked linen dress and polished leather shoes with rather higher than usual heels.

She is a citizen, indeed a Party member, of a small ellipsoid state in eastern Europe resembling in its dimensions a heaped-up apple tart viewed in profile. The top crust presses northward toward a sparsely populated mountainous area that still erupts from time to time with primitive vendettas whose roots go back to the time of the Turkish occupation. This is harsh terrain for the most part, with scanty soil and rough roads, but the southern corner of the geo-pie plate tilts onto a green curve of the Adriatic, and this short, favored stretch is about to be developed into a full-scale tourist facility. At present there is only a four-story concrete hostel suitable for the busloads of students or workers who have lately been encouraged to come here for their twenty-four-day vacation period. But the time for expansion has arrived; even in this part of the world people are talking foreign currency; foreign currency's the key. The beaches here are broad and breezy, and despite an overrun of tufted sea grass, the potential's unlimited. A recreational consultant, Malcolm Brownstone, is being sent, today, by an international cooperative agency to advise on the initial stages of development.

A mere thirty miles from this future fantasyland is the capital city where Martä Gjatä lives. Hers is a country often confused with toy principalities like Andorra and Monaco, but in fact is a complex ensemble of mountains and streambeds and rich deposits of iron and chromium and annual rainfall statistics going back to the year 1910. There are also some Roman ruins and a number of mosques, now turned into museums, and the busy capital city (pop. 200,000) where Martä and her mother and her mother's brother Miço live. (A fourth member of the household is old Zana, a family servant before Liberation, now lingering on as an honorary aunt and in winter sharing her bed with Uncle Miço, an *Ethnoggraphi Emerti* at the National University.) The apartment is small. The cooking facilities are rudimentary and the food somewhat monotonous, but Martä, aged forty-two, prides herself on creating a style to suit her confining circumstances. She makes a delicious *mjarzadjpër*, which is a mixture of cabbage, cheese and onions spiced with pepper. And the green checked dress she wears today is one she made herself.

She is a worker in the state film industry which last year produced fourteen feature films and more than twenty documentaries. She is also one of the few women to have been promoted to *Direktor*. This was three years ago. Before that time she was a celebrated film actress. *The Scent of Flowers* and *Glorious Struggle* are her most beloved films and the ones that have made her famous in her country. In the first of these she played the daughter of a patriot. She wore a kerchief and an embroidered apron (borrowed from Zana, since there was no such thing as a wardrobe department in the early days) and served glasses of raki to filthy, wounded soldiers, falling passionately in love with one of them, a mere boy whose legs had been crudely amputated after battle. (In real life this young man, Dimitro Puro, had been run over by a tractor.) The film closes with a village wedding scene (Dimitro and Martä) that is exuberantly folkloric but sadly muted by the spotty black and white film then in use, color film having been forbidden before the cultural revolution of 1979.

The cultural revolution lasted two days and consisted of a letter written by Martä Gjatä to the Minister of Kulture pleading for a change from black and white film to bourgeois color. Martä delivered the request herself, placing it in the Minister's hand and giving his wide cheek a playful pat. That was the first day. The next day she had her answer, a typed directive delivered to her apartment saying: "If you think the time has come, my darling Martä, then the time has come." Both letters were immediately destroyed, though they continue to exist as part of the biographical patrimony, along with all other gestures, events, and texts of this curious period. Biography works both sides of the street. Iron curtain, velvet curtain, it's all the same to biography.

In her final film, *Glorious Struggle*, Martä played the perplexed middle-aged mother–though she was herself still in her thirties–of a brilliant eighteen-year-old daughter who elects a career in Civil Engineering. The film was immensely popular, but was later criticized for its too obvious didacticism, its repetitive and ultimately tiresome plea for gender equality. Still, Martä's performance, her face passing through wider and wider rings of comprehension, raised it to the level of near-art, and there was talk for a time of international distribution. "No" came an order from higher–much higher–up. "Not yet."

A year ago the Minister of Kulture died. He and Martä had been lovers for some twenty years, but out of oversight or mutual evasion had not married. His death was caused by choking; a laurel leaf buried in a mutton stew caught in his throat. This was during a dinner at the Rumanian Embassy. He was not yet fifty, still a relatively young man with dark hair rising cleanly from a blank forehead. He might have grown beautiful with time; white hair might have given him distinction, putting edges on his large weak face and blunted features, connoting kindness or refinement. Maybe.

Martä was away at the time of his death, directing a documentary on the glass industry in the north of the country. This was not at all the kind of film she was used to working on, and the thought came to her that her lover had sent her away deliberately in order to get her out of the way. She has no proof of this, only a suspicion that confirms itself by a muttering inattention. She knows what she knows, just as her tongue apprehends the crenellations of her teeth but can't describe them. The love affair had grown desultory on both sides; occasionally she had felt herself straining to play refining fire to her lover's rather dainty brutality. "Little Martä," he often said, kissing her small breasts and giving a laugh that came out a snicker.

There is no laugh like a snicker. We want to cover our ears with shame and shut it out, but in biography the snicker lives on, a laugh trying to be a good laugh but not knowing how. Like radioactive ash or like the differentiated particles of luminescence that cling to the dark side of the globe, the chambered beginnings, middles and ends of human encounters persist, including aberrations, nervous tics and malfunctions of the spirit. A snicker cannot easily be disposed of, certainly not a habitual snicker, and thinking about her lover after his death, Martä is unable to imagine him without the stale accompaniment of snorting air. It condenses on her neck and eyes. Her remembrances taste of yellow metal, not nostalgia, and her lover's glum, puffy face continues to retreat behind a series of small puckered explosions. She did not return to the capital for his official interment and memorial ceremony, claiming quite rightly that the documentary on the glass industry must come first.

Glass has been manufactured in Martä's country only since the nineteen-fifties, before which time it was imported from Yugoslavia. The quality of domestic glass is poor. (Tumblers and wine glasses possess an ineradicable greenish tinge, and it has proven difficult to achieve quality control; household glassware is either too thick or too thin and often breaks the first time it's put into hot water.) But there has been considerable success with industrial glass, perhaps because a higher priority has been assigned, with the result that there is now a surplus of such products, and it has been decided to seek foreign markets. Hence the making of the documentary film.

Martä has always loved glass, and her biography is punctuated with references to the colors of glass, the clarity, the fluid shapes and artful irregularities, to the opaque glass grotto of her earliest memory, the time as a young child when she scratched her name, Martä Gjatä, on a frost-coated window, putting the scrapings of shirred ice on her tongue where they deliciously melted. Around her neck, on a fine chain, she wears a pendant of seaglass, a gift from the legless actor/soldier, now a translator of textbooks, who played opposite her in *The Scent of Flowers*. A shelf in her apartment holds an antique goblet of lead crystal brought back from Venice by the Minister of Kulture shortly before his death. When Martä flicks at it, hard, with her duster (a pair of old underpants), she is forced to balance the slack fleshiness of his face against their many tender hours of love, sometimes in the woods outside the city, sometimes very quietly on the dusty linoleum floor of a storeroom in the basement of the Palace of Kulture. She has time while dusting for her memories to bloom into flower silhouettes and glide slowly past her, a shadow parade with a cracked element of confusion. She's glad at these times that she has her work to distract her and deaden her thoughts.

The creation of the documentary presented certain structural problems, and these Martä solved by dividing the glass-making process into a series of elegant steps, and running beneath them a counter-process of poetic permutation that sent transparency flowing backward into elemental sand. She spent several weeks editing the footage, insisting on doing it herself, working even on Sunday, which was the day she had once spent walking in the woods outside the city with her lover. The work took her mind off the unfilled space ahead of her which seemed now, with its blocky weekends and solid uncomplicated months, too large to contain her small patient undertakings and too indifferent to provide the sort of convulsion she is secretly hoping for.

For its kind, the glass documentary is a success—thirty minutes of witty, visual exposition in which even the machinery of the glass factory seems to be smiling. It has already been dubbed into four languages, French, Italian, German, and English–not one of which Martä understands, languages being her single failing–and an illustrated catalog has been prepared. Martä has brought the catalogs to the Hotel Turista today where she will shortly be meeting a two-man trade delegation from Austria.

She is early, seated at a low, rather battered table, drinking coffee. Her cardboard satchel of film catalogs is on the floor beside her. From time to time she peers out the window through the lace curtains and sees that the blue sky is now blackened with cloud, what looks like forewarnings of rain. The Austrians apparently are still in the dining room, taking their time over lunch, and the coffee salon is empty except for Martä herself in her checked dress and, at the far end of the room, a bald-headed man bent heavily over a pile of papers. Martä glances in his direction and identifies him as a foreigner–there's a certain opacity about him, a largeness and lope to his shoulders and arms, and a visitor's face on his face–but she has no way of knowing who he is or why he's here.

The arrival of a Recreation and Resort Consultant (Malcolm Brownstone's official title) is a portent, a sign the country is opening up and welcoming the high-tech wizardry of the West. Even more remarkable is the notion of exploitable hedonism, a new idea in this country and one which Malcolm ironically represents (a biographical fault line here, since he is known to be a hard-working man of puritan tastes, but one whose last thirty years have been beamed in the direction of pleasure).

He is comfortable with the lace curtains in the Hotel Turista, more than comfortable; he loves them and is reminded of the small frame house where he grew up, a rented house with a curved brow of shingles and two upstairs windows like staring eyes. The house held many of the usual mid-continental variables: bibles, hairbrushes, folded blankets on shelves, an enamel breadbox with the word "bread" stamped on its hinged lid, a modest lean-bodied father with a mild passion for horseshoe pitching and a mother with a tinkling laugh and reserves of good health. There were two sisters, both of them scholarly, both of them pretty. The sisters, and Malcolm too, made the most of their opportunities, never suspecting that their opportunities were limited. They married, bore children, were rewarded and punished, sought friends, took vacations, saved their money, also spent it, and grew older, making regular compulsory deposits as they went along to biography's vast holdings.

Out of all this planetary chaff it might be thought that a mathematical model could be fashioned, an orderly super-bio whose laws and forms are predictable and reduced. But this is where anarchy enters in, or, depending on your perspective, systematic rebellion. At various times, for instance, it has been forbidden to eat tomatoes, to poach pheasants, to curse God, to strangle infants and to break promises. Still, people did these things and survived and contributed their chapters of anomaly and exception. The otherwise cases, the potent singularities–they also survive, along with precarious half-heard harmonies and the leaky disrepair of memory (Malcolm Brownstone's mystic experience on a Ferris wheel in

1947 when he observed curls of crisp gold raveling off the sun; Martä Gjatä's love letter–to a paraplegic film actor–which she later tore into forty-three pieces and hurled into a weedy pond).

One of Malcolm Brownstone's first undertakings as a young architect was the development of a "theme park" in a region of his own country that seemed to possess no outstanding characteristics (high unemployment figures notwithstanding), and very little in the way of historical resonance. There was nothing, *nothing*, he could draw on other than the longings of displaced agricultural workers to become once again solvent and respectable. These longings he translated into dreams, and thus Dreamland was born, a commercial wonder, then as now. It contains a Dream City, a Dream Palace, a Dream Mountain, a Dream-o-rama where Dreamobiles race along banked curves, and a Dream-Stream on which floats a Dreamboat commandeered by Dream Maids dispensing at reasonable prices such dream favors as Dreamy Candy Floss and Dreamy-Ice.

Wisely he bought shares and immediately incorporated himself, an act of biographical distortion in which a single life sometimes gives the impression of multiple tracks. He grew rich, which did not surprise him. What surprised him was his baldness at the age of thirty-five. His biography is starred with attempts to reconcile himself to his few last scurrying hairs and the melon of scalp rising above an eave of bone. He cannot pass a mirror, even today, without a stab of confusion–who is this person? Today at the airport he was met by an official car; the driver, he noticed, had a headful of thick, thrusting hair. The two of them drove silently past fields of cabbages and women with scarves wrapped around their heads leading donkeys down the road, but all he could see was the driver's strongly rooted hair and his own slicked skull bouncing whitely off the rear-view mirror.

He is an earnest man, an Organization man, but with the kind of dislocated piety that the Organization finds awkward. His ordered, monotone missions to marginal-economy countries are undertaken with unfashionable fervor. He wants, he says aloud, to help people. His sense of vocation arrived suddenly during a trip he and his wife took to North Africa in 1976. Standing in a village souk, his eyes traveled accidentally past a wool dyer's stall to the dark room beyond where he beheld an earthen floor and children who were of an age to be in school. He seemed to hear the words: "You are close to discovering a way to make life meaningful." A month later, in a mood of panic and high drama, he disincorporated himself–another bio blip–and joined the Organization as a dollar-a-year man.

His wife sniffled and wept. She hated to travel, to pack and unpack, to plug her hairdryer into complicated converters and risk danger. On one occasion she was startled by a large oily beetle that climbed out of a bath drain. She had frequent gastric upsets and skin rashes. Some of the countries where they were sent had unreliable water supplies and incomprehensible languages (neither she nor her husband had any aptitude for foreign languages) and systems of public morality that seemed whimsically derived from the demands of long-standing hunger.

Two years after Malcolm joined the Organization, his wife died of a stroke. Her last words before slipping into the coma that ended her life were, "You were always such a cold potato."

That's what he lives with, this icy epitaph–not even, in fact, true–and his awareness, always with him, of his scraped head. The two images overlap cruelly–potato/head–and churn him to action. Spareness, openness, bareness–these he avoids for the organized compression of public gathering places, parks and fairs, playgrounds and carnivals, pleasure domes and civic squares, the whole burning convivial world where he feels the massed volume of other lives. The truth is, though he doesn't realize it, there is not one corner of our cold green rocky world that isn't silted down by biography's buzzing accumulation. It's a wonder we can still breathe, a miracle we can still move about and carry on with the muffled linearity that stretches between the A of birth and the B of death. Malcolm Brownstone imagines that he is two-thirds along that mortal line, an alarming thought but also a comforting one.

Today, in the coffee salon of the Hotel Turista, he is joined by three *functionari* from the Ministry of Interior Development. They are all of them men with short necks and copious hair–is there no end to this hair?–and dressed alike in suits so dark that the folds of cloth are without shadows. Against Malcolm's vast beige wall of tweed they seem to merge one into the other. An interpreter is necessarily present. A very young woman, still a student, she has made an attempt at fashion by pinning a crocheted collar to a plain brown sweater. This collar she touches now and then as she transforms Malcolm's preliminary recommendations into the furze and petals and throaty moss of the national language. Her biographical density is powerful, since very little as yet has been expended, and it hurts Malcolm's heart to look at her, the way she fingers her collar and twists an earring as she exchanges the sprawled flowers of her native tongue for the thudding bricks of his own English.

It puzzles him, but only a little, that official business in this part of the world should be conducted in the homey, lace-curtained public rooms of hotels rather than in offices or boardrooms. He is not at all sure that such offices and boardrooms exist. But what does it matter, he asks himself, as long as progress is made.

And in the next two hours, between three-thirty and five-thirty, two small international agreements are reached, one in each end of the coffee salon. The room darkens subtly as though in acknowledgment. Raki is ordered and cakes are brought around.

To her Austrian visitors Martä Gjatä delivers nothing, promises nothing, but through a burly boy of an interpreter persuades them that their opportunities will be diminished if they return home without her explanatory brochures and a copy of her film which has been given the engaging title *Jepnï Nje Lutëm* (*A Gift of Brightness*).

Malcolm Brownstone has determinedly sold his vision to his hosts, assuring them that Pleasure with a capital P is the springboard not only of profit but of progress, that healthy relaxed bodies roasted by the sun and bathed in a benign sea are all the more ready to stand on guard for the State. Though he won't actually visit the site until the following morning, he has already studied the pertinent maps, charts, graphs, blueprints and photographs. He mentions matching funds, contract requirements, climate variables, the components of tide, wind, and hours of annual sunshine.

By chance or perhaps by some diminution of an electric charge running from one end of the room to the other, the two meetings break up at the same moment. The Austrian duo shakes hands with Martä and heads for the *boit de nuit* in the basement of the hotel where they will while away a few hours with green beer and illicit dancers. They kindly suggest that Martä join them, but she declines. She is expected at home, she says; she must catch her bus at the People's Square.

The three dark-suited *functionari*, through the medium of their blushing translator, bid good evening to their distinguished guest, Malcolm Brownstone. They wish him a pleasing night. They are sorry, they say, that the rain has spoiled the evening, but the countryside has been needing such a wetting. His suggestions have greatly animated them and they look forward to traveling with him on the morrow to the coast. A car will call for him at eight-thirty and it is hoped that this very hour is agreeable.

Badly translated languages fill Malcolm with sentiment, touching his primal sense of what a language should be, every word snugged in a net of greeting. He is charmed by inversions. He welcomes the derangement of grammar and the matching derangement of his senses. Affection surges. He would like to embrace these three chunky men, as well as the earnest translator who is now giggling helplessly and struggling into a raincoat. Instead he bows elegantly, like an oversized actor, and shakes hands all round. A minute later he finds himself, too suddenly, alone.

A walk is what he needs. A stroll on the Boulevard Skopjerlë, at dusk, at twilight, a look at the famous People's Square in the center of the city. Outside the rain is pouring down, but luckily in his briefcase he has a folding umbrella, a marvel of hinged ribs and compacted nylon. He never travels without it. At the wide front door of the hotel–marble flooring stained and splitting–he collides with Martä Gjatä. She salutes him with her droll eyes and the smallest of shrugs. *Rain* is what her look says, *rain and me without an umbrella*. She bites her lower lip and smiles.

The smile might mean anything. Malcolm interprets it as the spasm of tension that often follows a moment of disconnection. He feels the same tension himself, and so returns the smile, but doubles the kilowatts. A real smile; no cold potato here, but a man of warmth and spontaneity; charming, helpful.

Not only does Martä not have her umbrella with her, she has no raincoat, not even a square of plastic to tie around her head. She doesn't mind about this. It's the cardboard briefcase she's worrying about; will it melt away in this deluge, and what about the rest of the brochures? They'll be ruined. She takes a tentative step forward, one high-heeled shoe advancing through the doorway and onto the flooded marble steps, then quickly retreats to the dry lobby.

Ssschwippp–the noise of an umbrella unfurling, Malcolm's made-in-Montreal umbrella; a cunning button pressed, and *voilà!* He gestures broadly at Martä and then at the umbrella. His forehead is working rhythmically, saying the unsayable in lines of brow.

In response Martä swings a dramatic arm in the

direction of the open door, a perennial actress with unstartled eyes and a cheerful shrug of complicity. She points to the cardboard valise, *helpless, helpless*, and pulls a rueful face.

Time to take charge. Malcolm nods northward in the direction of the People's Square. A query, a proposition. He touches his tweed chest, a vigorous me-too sign and, with surprising delicacy for such a large person, mimes the classic gesture of invitation, a hand uncurled, beckoning, one finger leading and the others following quickly. Why not? his look says.

Why not? Martä mimes back. No coyness here, not at age forty-two, not from a woman whose biography drills straight through to struggle and achievement and recent pools of terrible loneliness. She ducks under the umbrella and together they set off, down the broad marble steps, a turn to the right smoothly performed, and then along the wide pavement skirting the boulevard.

"You a visitor here also?" asks Malcolm, shouting above the noise of battering rain and reverting to the wooden English he uses when visiting foreign countries.

"Ko yon skoni?" Martä asks, waving a pretty arm, baring her teeth.

"A rainy night," Malcolm says loudly.

"Por farë feni (with great pleasure)," Martä replies.

They both stop suddenly and smile. The futility of language. The impossibility.

Hundreds of people fill the street, some of them running, only a few equipped with umbrellas, most of them comically drenched. Who would have thought the weather would turn so suddenly! Men, women and children. The end of the working day. Everyone seems to be carrying a bundle of some sort, vegetables or kindling or books, and these they attempt to shield from the downpour. Under Malcolm's strong black umbrella Martä and her cardboard case stay dry. She has given up on conversation; so has Malcolm.

They step with care. Portions of the boulevard have been smoothed with concrete, but in other places the old cobbles poke through, making the surface tricky, especially for Martä in her high-heeled shoes. In order to keep her balance (and because it is difficult for a short woman to walk with a tall man under an umbrella) she takes Malcolm's arm. Not a bold gesture, not at all, but a forthcoming one, also intimate. It is likely that Malcolm extended his elbow slightly by way of entreaty–half a centimeter would have done it, would have given permission; an old-worldly habit to walk arm-in-arm, emphatically neutral but with a ripple of protective tribute.

The distance between the Hotel Turista and the People's Square is only a kilometer, a mere stroll, 0.6 of a mile. The rain grows more intense, but instead of hurrying them along, it slows them down. First Malcolm must adjust his long steps to match Martä's and, after a minute or two of faltering, of amused back and forth glances, they find their ideal stride, a strolling, rolling gait, right and left, right and left. Malcolm brings his elbow closer to his body so that the back of Martä's tucked hand is in contact with the large damp paleness of his jacket. There it stays, there it fuses.

Ahead of them the lights of the People's Square blink unsteadily. It is the slashing of the rain that gives this look of unsteadiness. Lights seen through a whorl of weather throb rather than shine, producing a rhythmic pulse that is always trying to mend itself but never catching up. Martä and Malcolm are locked together by this rhythm, left and right, left and right, one body instead of two. If only they could walk like this forever. Malcolm has spent his whole life arriving at this moment; this is the best bit of walking he's ever going to do, and it seems to last and last, one quarter-hour unfolding into a measureless present.

Martä, dazed by a distortion of time and light, thinks how this round black umbrella gives an unasked-for refuge, how the rain becomes a world in itself, how the kilometer of rutted city street has become a furrow of love. It will never end, she thinks, knowing it is about to.

Biography, that old buzzard, is having a field day, running along behind them picking up all the bits and pieces. Biography is used to kinks and wherewithal, it expects to find people in odd pockets, it's used to surges of speechless passion that come out of nowhere and sink without a murmur. It doesn't care. It doesn't even have the decency to wait until Martä and Malcolm get to the People's Square, shake hands, go their separate ways and resume their different versions of time travel, not to collide again. This isn't one of Martä's movies, this is life. This is biography. Nothing matters except for the harvest, the gathering in, the adding up, the bringing together, the whole story, the way it happens and happens and goes on happening.

Good Manners

The stern, peremptory social arbiter, Georgia Willow, has been overseeing Canadian manners for thirty-five years. She did it in Montreal during the tricky fifties and she did it in Toronto in the unsettled sixties. In the seventies she operated underground, so to speak, from a converted Rosedale garage, tutoring the shy wives of Japanese executives and diplomats. In the eighties she came into her own; manners were rediscovered, particularly in the West where Mrs. Willow has relocated.

Promptly at three-thirty each Tuesday and Thursday, neatly dressed in a well-pressed navy Evan-Picone slub silk suit, cream blouse, and muted scarf, Georgia Willow meets her small class in the reception area of the MacDonald Hotel and ushers them into the long, airy tearoom–called, for some reason,

Gophers–where a ceremonial spread has been ordered.

Food and drink almost always accompany Mrs. Willow's lectures. It is purely a matter of simulation since, wherever half a dozen people gather, there is sure to be a tray of sandwiches to trip them up. According to Mrs. Willow, food and food implements are responsible for fifty per cent of social unease. The classic olive pit question. The persisting problem of forks, cocktail picks, and coffee spoons. The more recent cherry-tomato dilemma. Potato skins, eat them or leave them? Saucers, the lack of. The challenge of the lobster. The table napkin quandary. Removing parsley from between the teeth. On and on.

There are also sessions devoted to hand-shaking, door-opening and rules regarding the wearing and nonwearing of gloves. And a concluding series of seminars on the all-important *langue de la politesse*, starting with the discourse of gesture, and moving on quickly to the correct phrase for the right moment, delivered with spiritual amplitude or imprecation or possibly something in between. Appropriateness is all, says Georgia Willow.

Our *doyenne* of good manners takes these problems one by one. She demonstrates and describes and explains the acceptable alternatives. She's excellent on fine points, she respects fine points. But always it's the philosophy *behind* good manners that she emphasizes.

Never forget, she tells her audience, what manners are *for*. Manners are the lubricant that eases our passage through life. Manners are the means by which we deflect evil. Manners are the first-aid kit we carry out on to the battlefield. Manners are the ceremonial silver tongs with which we help ourselves to life's most alluring moments.

She says these things to a circle of puzzled faces. Some of those present take notes, others yawn; all find it difficult to deal with Mrs. Willow's more exuberant abstractions. As a sensitive person, she understands this perfectly well; she sympathizes and, if she were less well-mannered, would illustrate her philosophy with personal anecdotes culled from her own experience. Like everyone else, her life has been filled with success and failure, with ardor and the lack of ardor, but she is not one of those who spends her time unpicking the past, blaming and projecting and drawing ill-bred conclusions or dragging out pieces of bloodied vision or shame. She keeps her lips sealed about personal matters and advises her clients to do the same. Nevertheless, certain of her experiences refuse to dissolve. They're still on center stage, so to speak, frozen tableaux waiting behind a thickish curtain.

Only very occasionally do they press their way forward and demand to be heard. She is ten years old. It is an hour before dusk on a summer evening. The motionless violet air has the same density and permanence as a word she keeps tripping over in story books, usually on the last page, the word *forever.* She intuitively, happily, believes at this moment that she will be locked forever into the simplicity of the blurred summer night, forever throwing a rubber ball against the forever side of her house and disturbing her mother with the sound of childish chanting. It is impossible for her to know that the adult world will someday, and soon, carry her away, reject her thesis on the *Chanson de*

Roland and the particular kind of dated beauty her features possess; that she will be the protagonist of an extremely unpleasant divorce case and, in the end, be forced to abandon a studio apartment on the twenty-fourth floor of an apartment building in a city two thousand miles from the site of this small wooden house; that she will feel in her sixtieth year as tired and worn down as the sagging board fence surrounding the house where she lives as a child, a fence that simultaneously protects and taunts her ten-year-old self.

On the other side of the fence is old Mr. Manfred, sharpening his lawnmower. She puts down her ball and watches him cautiously, his round back, his chin full of gray teeth, the cloud of white hair resting so lazily on top of his head, and the wayward, unquenchable dullness of his eyes. Twice in the past he has offered her peppermints, and twice, mindful of her mother's warnings, she has refused. "No, thank you," she said each time. But it had been painful for her, saying no. She had felt no answering sense of virtue, only the hope that he might offer again.

Tonight Mr. Manfred walks over to the fence and tells her he has a secret. He whispers it into her ear. This secret has a devious shape: grotesque flapping ears and a loose drooling mouth. Mr. Manfred's words seem ghosted by the scent of the oil can he holds in his right hand. In his left hand, in the folds of his cotton work pants, he grasps a tube of pink snouty dampish flesh. What he whispers is formlessly narrative and involves the familiar daylight objects of underwear and fingers and the reward of peppermint candy.

But then he draws back suddenly as though stung

by a wasp. The oil can rolls and rolls and rolls on the ground. He knows, and Georgia, aged ten, knows that something inadmissible has been said, something that cannot be withdrawn. Or can it? A dangerous proposition has been placed in her hand. It burns and shines. She wants to hand it back quickly, get rid of it somehow, but etiquette demands that she first translate it into something bearable.

The only other language she knows is incomprehension, and luckily she's been taught the apt phrase. "I beg your pardon?" she says to Mr. Manfred. Her face does a courteous twist, enterprising, meek, placatory, and masked with power, allowing Mr. Manfred time to sink back into the lavender twilight of the uncut grass. "I'm afraid I didn't quite hear. . . . "

Later, twenty-three years old, she is on a train, the Super Continental, traveling eastward. She has a window seat, and sunlight gathers around the crown of her hair. She knows how she must look, with her thin clever mouth and F. Scott Fitzgerald eyes.

"I can't resist introducing myself," a man says.

"Pardon?" She is clearly flustered. He has a beautiful face, carved cheeks, crisp gray hair curling at the forehead.

"The book," he points. "The book you're reading. It looks very interesting."

"Ah," she says.

Two days later they are in bed together, a hotel room, and she reflects on the fact that she has not finished the book, that she doesn't care if she ever does, for how can a book above love compare with what she now knows.

"I'm sorry," he says then. "I hadn't realized I was the first."

"Oh, but you're not," she cries.

This curious lie can only be accounted for by a wish to keep his love. But it turns out she has never had it, not for one minute, not love as she imagines it.

"I should have made things clear to you at once," he says. How was he to know she would mistake a random disruption for lasting attachment? He is decent enough to feel ashamed. He only wanted. He never intended. He has no business. If only she.

She seems to hear cloth ripping behind her eyes. The syntax of culpability—he's drowning in it, and trying to drown her too. She watches him closely, and the sight of his touching, disloyal mouth restores her composure. Courtesy demands that she rescue him and save herself at the same time. This isn't shrewdness talking, this is good manners, and there is nothing more economical, she believes, than the language of good manners. It costs nothing, it's portable, easy to handle, malleable, yet pre-formed. Two words are all that are required, and she pronounces them slippingly, like musical notes. "Forgive me," she says.

There. It's said. Was that so hard?

There is a certain thing we must all have, as Georgia Willow has learned in the course of her long life. We may be bankrupt, enfeebled, ill or depraved, but we must have our good stories, our moments of vividness. We keep our door closed, yes, and move among our scratched furniture, old photographs, calendars and keys, ticket stubs, pencil ends and lacquered trays, but in the end we'll wither away unless we have a little human attention.

But no one seems to want to give it away these days, not to Georgia Willow. It seems she is obliged to ask even for the unpunctual treats of human warmth. A certain amount of joyless groping is required and even then it's hard to get enough. It is especially painful for someone who, after all, is a personage in her country. She has her pride, her reputation–and a scattering of small bruise-colored spots on the back of her long thin hands. It makes you shudder to think what she must have to do, what she has to say, how she is obliged to open her mouth and say *please.*

Please is a mean word. A word in leg irons. She doesn't say it often. Her pleases and thank-yous are performed in soft-focus, as they like to say in the cinema world. It has nothing to do with love, but you can imagine how it is for her, having to ask and then having to be grateful. It's too bad. Good manners had such a happy childhood, but then things got complicated. The weave of complication has brought Georgia Willow up against those she would not care to meet again, not in broad daylight anyway, and others who have extracted far more than poor Mr. Manfred at the garden fence ever dreamed of. Good manners are not always nice, not nice at all, although Mrs. Willow has a way of banishing the hard outlines of time and place, and of course she would never think of naming names. Discretion is one of her tenets. She does a special Monday afternoon series on discretion in which she enjoins others to avoid personal inquiries and pointed judgments.

"Courtesy," concludes Georgia Willow, "is like the golden coin in the princess's silk purse. Every time it's spent worthily, another appears in its place."

Almost everyone agrees with her. However much they look into her eyes and think she is uttering mere niceties, they are sworn to that ultimate courtesy which is to believe what people want us to believe. And thus, when Mrs. Willow bids them good afternoon, they courteously rise to their feet. "Good afternoon," they smile back, shaking hands carefully, and postponing their slow, rhythmic applause and the smashing of the teacups.

Times of Sickness and Health

Kay's mother had ideas, notions of refinement. One of these notions was that young girls benefitted from the experience of ballet classes, and so all three of her daughters were enrolled–Kay's sister Joan, a second sister Dorrie, and Kay herself who was the youngest in the class, the youngest by far, being not quite five years old.

The lessons were held in a large mirrored room on the second floor of a commercial building. Kay remembers the long unbroken stairway, lit at the top and bottom, but dark in the middle. Their dance shoes they carried in their hands, soft-toed satiny slippers, not the hard-nosed shoes of classical ballet. The teacher was a thin, darkish woman. She wore a kind of short-skirted costume. Fancy, shiny. Another woman played the piano. One-two-three-jump was the way they started off each week.

The older girls seemed able to remember the order of the dance steps. Kay watched them hard, baffled by their ease and earnestness, trying to copy what their arms and feet did, but she was unable to shake off a sense of dazed confusion. There was dust on the mirror walls and on the hardwood floor. What was she doing here? It seemed to go on for a very long time, over and over again, one-two-three-jump.

There was mention of a recital. It filtered through to Kay, that charmed, important word. *Recital.* Like ice in a pitcher of water. The class was perfecting a dance routine called "The Wedding," and Kay's sister, Joan, was appointed the bride, a deserved tribute it seemed. Everyone else was to be a brides-maid, except for Kay who was given the role of flower girl. She had no idea what this meant. She'd seen her mother cover her hands with flour when she made pie crust, smooth it on her fingers and palms, rub it into the rolling pin and on the pastry board.

A small berry basket filled with torn-up bits of newspaper was put in Kay's hands. These she was to scatter on the floor during the course of the wedding dance. This crude, stained basket with its improvised string handle and its rubbishy contents spelled out the fullness of her disgrace. Clearly she was being punished, but why? She did as she was told, shuffled and kicked and turned, always a shameful half-second behind the others, and threw paper on the floor, knowing she was doomed and powerless. Something was wrong, but she didn't know what.

Who would she have asked? And what would she have said?

Kay, who is fifty, has no children of her own, but is interested in the way children think and the questions they like to ask. For example: is a tomato a fruit or a vegetable? (Which is it?–Kay's looked it up but can't remember.) Do these querying children, she wonders, really want an answer? Or is there a kind of hopeful rejoicing at the overlapping of categories, a suggestion that the material and immaterial world spills out beyond its self-imposed classifications? What is the difference between sand and gravel? Between weeds and flowers? Between liking and loving?

It occurs to her that these children may be bluffing with their bright, winning curiosity, being playful and sly, and masking a deeper, more abject and injurious sense of bewilderment. There is, after all, so much authentic chaos to sort out, so much seething muddle and predicament that it is a wonder children survive their early ignorance. How do they bear it? You would think they would hold their breath out of sheer rage or hurl themselves down flights of stairs. You would think they'd get sick and die.

"Do you know Philip Halliwell?" a woman asked Kay.

Kay was a young woman, barely more than a girl,

standing in a public washroom applying lipstick, the ruby red putty people wore in those days.

"Slightly," she answered carefully.

"I wouldn't trust him further than I could throw him," the woman said.

Kay slipped quickly past a row of women who were saying things women had always said. The same things their mothers and grandmothers have said, shaking the same powder across their broad or narrow noses and peering at their dabbed, genetically condemned faces or at a broken nail, probably bitten, held up and examined in the weak light. No, she did not trust Philip Halliwell. But she had fallen under his spell. That's what it felt like, being under a spell. She had, in fact, after a two-week courtship, married him. It was a secret marriage because she was still a student, working in the field of early English manuscripts. She lived in a women's residence and held a prestigious scholarship which would have been jeopardized, or so they reasoned. All this was years and years ago.

Recently she was in the hospital for a week (tests, bone scans, which turned out negative, thank God) and Philip sent a basket of hydrangea. She hadn't seen him for six months, and so the gift surprised her. But she didn't know how to look after these particular flowers, and the nurses were too rushed off their feet to lend a hand. She took the nearly dead plant home, and on the way through the hospital corridor two people stopped her and instructed her in the care of hydrangeas. "Never let the roots go dry," one said. The other said, "Water daily, but don't allow the roots to actually stand in water."

Many people resent advice, and Kay has never

been able to understand this. A man she knows, Nils Almquist, a cataloger in the museum where she works, tells her that this resistance to advice is a Teutonic failing, that people from Mediterranean countries–Greece, Italy, Spain–routinely ask the advice of their friends and relatives before making a major decision. It is a sign of courtesy to seek counsel. People whose opinion is sought are flattered, and at the same time no one is strictly bound to accept what is offered. This arrangement strikes Kay as having a good deal of human flexibility to it, and a crafty balance of consolation and hoarded-up responsibility.

"Never wear white pumps after Labor Day," her mother used to say, "or before the twenty-fourth of May." Kay believed this. It made a kind of sense, these permissive bracketing holidays and the broad field of liberty that lay between. "If you lose something," a girl named Patsy Tobin told her when she was about seven or eight, "just shut your eyes and pray to St. Anthony." Patsy Tobin's family was Roman Catholic, which was why she knew of the secret and specialized powers of St. Anthony. The advice worked. After uttering a short, breathy prayer ("Dear St. Anthony, please help me find. . ."), Kay almost always came across her lost shoe or doll or handkerchief or whatever. "When you have the growing pains in your legs," her Auntie Ruth said during one of her prolonged summer visits, "lie very still in bed, not moving a muscle, and count to one hundred." This proved excellent advice, practical to the point of magic, for not only did the pains ease as she counted, but she was almost always fast asleep before reaching a hundred.

"Happiness is capability." A woman Kay knows has written this sentence on a slip of paper and stuck it to her refrigerator door with one of those little magnets. "Oh, I know it sounds simplistic," she said, reading Kay's expression, "but it works. And it's the only thing that does work."

"There must be something you can do for him," Kay said to the doctor when her father lay dying–bedridden, bored, kept from his pinochle and poker cronies–in terrible pain. She had arranged the post-ponement of her comprehensive exams and come home for a few weeks.

"Aside from boiling up a deck of cards and feeding him the broth, we can't do a thing," the doctor said.

She liked this brand of non-advice. She found it ironic, indirect, cocky and kindly meant. It seemed like the sort of folksy palliative you might hear from a grunty old family practitioner. But this was a young doctor speaking. A very tall, good looking man with exceptionally blue eyes. Kay had only just met him that morning. His name, he told her, was Philip. They shook hands and then he helped her on with her coat. She looked tired, he said, especially her eyes.

For some reason–self-pity or injured vanity–this made her want to lean up against him and cry, but she remembers that she resisted.

Her father did not die, not then. Instead he made something of a limited recovery, getting out of bed eventually, getting himself dressed, taking short walks in the neighborhood, going as far as the corner for a newspaper or a loaf of bread. His clothes hung loosely on him, looked clownish and poor, and Kay wondered at that time why her mother didn't do something about those miserable clothes. He had given up smoking at the start of his illness; now he gave up cards. If he came upon a group of men hunched over a game, he shook his head in a puzzled but unreproachful way as though powerless to understand why grown men would idle away valuable time.

He started to read a thick book about butterflies. Kay remembers that her mother bought this book in a second-hand store; she was always haunting such places. She loved a bargain. The book was old, its cover damaged, but the color plates were in beautiful condition. Better still, here and there, preserved in the pages close to the spine, were the dried pressed bodies of real butterflies, captured by some previous reader. They were exceedingly fragile but had kept their color and, like thin sheets of mica, glinted with metallic richness. When her father came across one of these flattened creatures, he left it where it was, untouched, as if it were a sign of good luck.

About this time Kay and Philip went to Sardinia. This was their so-called honeymoon, delayed nearly two years because of her father's condition and also because of revisions to her thesis. It was a terrible day when they left, an afternoon in late January. It was necessary to land in Toronto in order to de-ice the plane. They taxied into a hangar where the whole of the plane–the wings, body and nose–was covered with pink foam. Kay remembers it took more than an hour to restore the plane's silvery sides, and even then they rose with a shudder into a gray, torn-up looking sky. It seemed not all that improbable that they would perish. Philip ordered a bottle of champagne somewhere over Quebec, Kay's first taste of champagne, though she was twenty-five years old at the time, a tall, loping, solemn girl with a head full of roughly filed facts and opinions.

Crossing the Atlantic, Philip ignored her. He had struck up an acquaintance with a Belgian priest across the aisle, and the two of them were soon trading anecdotes—miracles and blessings of a medical and spiritual nature. Half-dozing, Kay listened to Philip describe the spontaneous recovery of one of his patients. It took a minute or two to realize it was her father's case he was recounting, the story was that full of echoes, pauses and resonance; her father with his flapping, shabby clothes became a kind of golden fabulation, a character in a rich folktale who had burst through to reality and health.

She has only a few memories of that time in Sardinia, and even the half-dozen, utterly faded, stiff-edged Polaroid snaps that remain seem to bear no relation to the two of them or what they hoped to find there: he sitting on a large rock with his hands stretched skyward; she in the doorway of a hotel; he stepping gracefully through the arch of an ancient chapel; she climbing into a little hump-backed rental car; he standing in the morning surf and wearing a pair of exotically printed swimming trunks; and another of him crouched on a hillside examining a small plant.

An odd thing happened. During the weeks in Sardinia they stayed in three different hotels, and in each of these places they were given the same room number, number five. Kay was the one who pointed this out to Philip, who might otherwise not have noticed. As a coincidence it seemed to her mildly amusing and, perhaps, even an omen of good luck, not that her instincts leaned toward omens. Philip, on the other hand, found it thrilling and also alarming. He brooded about the numbers and even quizzed the desk clerk in the third hotel about the way in which rooms were allotted. Though their time was running out, he insisted on registering in a fourth hotel in order to test the pattern, then changed his mind at the last minute. One night he worked out the probability figures on the back of a menu, allowing each hotel fifteen rooms. The numbers were overwhelmingly against such a coincidence. He rechecked the figures. "Look at this," he demanded. Kay could see that he felt threatened and at the same time exhilarated. He discussed it with anyone who would listen including, one evening, a British couple they met in the hotel dining room. His voice grew implausibly overpitched, and the English pair exchanged sharp looks of apprehension–or so Kay thought. The next morning he woke up saying, "I'm making too much of this. I'm letting it get to me."

In Kay's memory the two of them took picnic lunches every day to lonely little beaches, but it may have been only two or three times that they did this. Probably they bought what they needed in the village shops, bread and sausage and a bottle of cheap wine. Kay remembers that one day–this was perhaps the same day Philip was cured of his obsession with the room numbers–they lay on their backs on the warm sand and she felt something brush her knee. It was a butterfly, not large, but quite brilliantly colored in shades of red and yellow and amber. She thought of her father's book and its brightly illustrated pages. Between the windows of color on the wings were tiny transparent panes edged in black. She held perfectly still, wondering what this creature made of the roundness of her knee, wondering if it perceived its own ephemeral grace. "Maybe it's a rare mutation," she said to Philip who had fallen asleep. "Maybe it's the world's rarest butterfly."

This seemed possible. She was not just being whimsical. Almost anything she could imagine seemed possible and, for the moment at least, she felt she knew everything she needed to know to stay alive in the world.

"The world's yours, honey, if you want it," Kay's Auntie Ruth used to say. Auntie Ruth was her mother's younger sister. She arrived every June for a visit and stayed until the first of August, sometimes longer if she judged she was not getting on her brother-in-law's nerves. For his part he was fond of her, but found her noisy chattering tiresome, and objected in a mild, manly way to her many toiletries lined up along the toilet tank. Kay's mother defended this array of lotions and powders; Auntie Ruth suffered from eczema, also heat rash and various unidentified allergies. Besides, she got it all for free since her husband, Uncle Nat, was a pharmacist.

Uncle Nat was left at home in Brandon. He was too tied down with the drugstore, Auntie Ruth maintained, to go for a vacation. He wasn't one for travel anyway, being older than Auntie Ruth, twenty years older, and suffering from piles and also backache. She, and Kay's mother too, referred to him as The Old Poke. "I'd better drop a few lines to The Old Poke," she would say a week or so into her visit.

Auntie Ruth's visits had an effect on Kay's mother; they made her girlish. The two of them set up folding cots on the screened porch so they could talk half the night away. They made themselves twin cotton dresses with wide circular skirts and wore them downtown. Once they dipped gumdrops in lemon extract, arranged them on top of a chiffon cake and set them alight at the table. Another day they dropped in on an old friend of Kay's mother who told them she had had an exhausting morning–she had rinsed out her shoe laces and brushed her teeth. They couldn't stop laughing at this, repeating it time and again and inventing variations. "I'm so tired, I just washed my feet and ironed a hanky." "I'm just done in, I've blown my nose and changed my underpants." On and on they went. Afternoons in the back yard, drinking glasses of iced tea, they speculated on their niece Ethel's hurry-up marriage. "You only have to put two and two together," Kay's mother said knowingly. "You only have to put *one* and *one* together," Auntie Ruth hooted, pitching them into spasms of hilarity.

At the end, though, there was trouble between them. Kay's mother lay in the hospital for four months with cancer of the lungs, this despite the fact that she had never smoked a cigarette in her life. Her sister Ruth sent her a card every single day, but in all those months she never once came to visit. "I can't, honey," she said to Kay on the telephone, speaking up because of the long distance. "Since your Uncle

Nat passed on I just can't face hospitals, they get me down so." Kay's mother refused at last to open the cards. She was bitter. She made her daughters promise they would have nothing to do with Auntie Ruth in the future, and they did promise. But, in fact, it was a promise that none of them has kept, or ever intended to.

It grieved Kay, though, that her mother should die with her heart hardened and set. She seemed to have forgotten all the good times, how the two sisters, she and Auntie Ruth, would move the sewing machine out on the porch and, in the space of an afternoon, recover a chair or make a new set of kitchen curtains. They made these things for almost nothing, cutting them out of remnants they scrambled for in back-street fabric outlets.

Kay's mother sewed beautifully, but considered herself a novice beside her younger sister. "Anyone can do plain sewing," she would say, "but your Auntie Ruth is a genius with the needle." Then she went misty-eyed with recollection. "Remember the year she came early to help with the ballet costumes? For the recital? They were tricky as can be, those little satin insets and the netting on the hats and at the wrists. Itchy to work with too, especially in hot weather. We worked right down to the wire. But we got them done."

"I don't remember," Kay said.

This was not true–she did remember, but saying she didn't was a way to strike out at her mother, letting her know she distrusted the touched-up trivia that formed the bulk of her remembrances and the treacly voice she used when invoking them. "I don't remember." She said it harshly, tossing it off.

"Well," her mother said, wistful, "you were very young. Just a baby. Probably too young to get anything much out of ballet lessons."

There was a coolness between them at this time because of Philip. Her mother had taken Kay aside. She had things to say to her. Handsome men, she said, can bring about problems in a marriage. They think they can go their own way. They get spoiled by flattery, by women falling about them. This leads to a lack of responsibility on their part. You can't count on them, and that's what marriage is in the long run, two people counting on each other, in good times and bad as it says in the wedding service, always having, no matter what, that one person in the world you can turn to.

The trouble was, this wasn't advice she was giving. It was prophecy. And already too late.

Kay has always believed herself fortunate in having sisters. Her sister, Joan, white-haired, heavy in the hips, already several times a grandmother, lets her talk on and on. She thinks it does her good, and it does. Kay's other sister Dorrie is equally sympathetic, but has a different style. She prods and interrupts and brings up tricky points. "What do you mean he forgets you?" she asked once. "Do you mean just birthdays and anniversaries and so on?"

That too, but much, much more. Once he met an old friend in a restaurant and they decided to fly to Whitehorse just like that. He phoned her the next day to let her know.

"Once," Dorrie pronounced, shrugging. "A lapse." Then asked, "And other women?"

Of course there were other women, almost from the start, but that wasn't really the problem. "He forgets I exist. Who I am. He looks at me but sees the wallpaper. He's courtly in the wrong way, like a man on automatic pilot. Even in bed–"

"Yes?"

Kay hadn't meant to get into this. "Even then I feel him slipping away. His arms are around me, yes, but his head's somewhere else. We might as well be in different rooms."

Kay also has long, frequent talks with her good friend Nils Almquist. Two or three times a month they have a drink together after work, around the corner at a place called The Laughing Moose. They favor a special table near a bank of potted begonias. Nils is every bit as good looking as Philip, but built along different lines, and Kay is about ninety-five per cent sure he's gay. She can tell him almost anything. He's one of those unusual people without twitches, able to sit for long periods of time with his body still and solid. It's this, she thinks, that encourages her confidences. One night not long ago she told him about Philip's final leaving, how he slipped off without a word, as though he'd suddenly remembered he had another existence elsewhere. How had she known it was the last time? Because of a sense of lightness that stole over her. To herself she said, almost laughing, "Well, that's that." She felt like someone getting up out of a sick bed, all her bones stiff but still in working order.

Besides her sisters and Nils and other assorted friends, she belongs to a weekly conversation group.

A talk circle is the official term. This group meets at Trinity Church Hall on Monday nights in a room furnished with easy chairs and soft lights.

Some years earlier, when things were going badly, she had come across a little printed notice that said: "Feeling alone and alienated? Coffee and conversation may be the answer."

She feared the usual unctuous welcoming remarks, braced herself for forced joviality and whining accord. Normally she was scornful of such endeavors, preferring to believe that liberal, educated people, nurtured from the cradle on communication skills, had no need for such organized embarrassment.

At the first meeting the discussion centered on the subject of favorite smells. One woman said moth balls. Another said coffee just after you grind the beans. A man said old ice skates when you bring them up from the basement. Kay said the smell of new cloth spread on a table, before you pin a pattern to it. The moth ball woman said yes, that was hers too, only she hadn't thought to mention it. She and Kay became close friends. It's she who has "Happiness is capability" on her refrigerator door.

Ecology is a frequent topic of discussion on these Monday nights, how to live more naturally and harmoniously in the world. Also the problem of public responsibility and private yearnings, the question of tolerance and instinct, or the spiritual self versus the material world.

But when things get too serious someone in the group will say, "Aren't we getting a bit heavy here?" and for a while they'll retreat to the primary edge and talk about such things as My Most Trying

Moment or The Book That Has Meant the Most to Me or My Favorite Color and Why. Last week they talked about My Earliest Memory.

Kay described the dance recital. By some trick of inversion this memory precedes the rehearsals themselves.

The recital was held in a new, strange place, not the big mirrored room with the dusty floor. Kay was told to wait in a dark place behind heavy curtains. She was shushed by one of the bigger girls, told to stand still or she'd rip her costume, and someone else handed her a large golden basket. Not real gold, but a graceful willow basket, probably spray painted; the handle was twisted and elegant and fit smoothly over the crook of Kay's arm. A whisper welled up: "Isn't she darling!" "Yes."

Then somebody, her sister Joan probably, gave her a push forward, whispering, "One-two-three-jump," and the next minute they were filing onto a small stage beyond which was nothing but a row of blinding lights and a wall of darkness. The darkness was false, full of held breath and heated expectations, that much Kay could understand.

A number of things seemed wrong. Her dance shoes made a different wash-wash sound on the slippery floor. There was a worrying sense of crowding and falling, and dazzle from the lights. Nevertheless she kept her eyes on the others, tried to do what they did, and reached, when the time came, into her basket. But what was this? This fragrant silky handful? Whatever it was fluttered upward into the air, a rounded spray of particles that drifted soundlessly to the floor. Again and then again.

There was too much surprise in this, too much of

shock and disorder. She observed the cascade of waxy pink and white flakes as they slipped from the angle of her hand, falling on the floor and on the toes of her shoes, and at last identified what they were.

The flower petals, the enchanting basket, her own exalted role, so unexpected–none of these things diminished in any way the humiliation she felt. She had been tricked, caught in a loop of incomprehension, given the hard slap of adult license. Adults were allowed to fool children, to withhold vital information, and this insult was sealed by the banked thunder of anonymous applause, as dense, unstartled and indiscriminate as the applause that comes out of a radio. Still she curtsied and smiled, feeling sick with shame.

Sick, Kay tells the Monday night group, and when she says sick, she means sick. She means weakness, fever, dizziness, shock, shortness of breath, all the fearful symptoms, but she had curtsied and smiled nevertheless.

Consciousness narrowed down to the width of her small hand in front of her face and the little dot of false light floating over the audience that she was unable to blink away.

But she stared straight ahead and willed herself to hold steady for a few seconds longer. Already she knew she would recover.

Family Secrets

Acres of corn, wheat fields and oats led right up to the town of DeKalb, Illinois, where there was a state normal school that prepared farm girls to go out and become school teachers, one of them being my young mother. This was not long after the First World War. She was sent first to teach in a four-room school in a place called Cortland where she stayed for two years. Why only two years? I must have asked her this at one time, or else my brother Barclay did. "I got sick," she said, "and had to go home for a while."

Where did she go? She went back to the forty-acre farm near Lemond where her mother and father lived, and after a year she got a job teaching on the west side of Chicago where she soon met our father and got married and began her real life.

I've thought lately about that time of sickness;

what kind of sickness is it that makes a young woman leave a job and go home to her parents for a whole year? The last time I saw Barclay I said to him, "I think Mom must have got pregnant that year she had to quit her first job."

It took him a minute to figure out what I was talking about. For a man so intelligent he has a poor memory for the details of our childhood. Once I tested him on the color of the garage doors we had at home in Maywood. "Blue," he said. "No," I shot back, "brown."

I had to remind him about Mom leaving the school in Cortland. I had to trot out the whole story, and then he leaned back and smiled his off-focus smile and said, oh yes, now he remembered.

"Well," I said, "what's your honest opinion? Do you think she got herself in trouble, as they used to say in those days?"

He shook his moony face. "I doubt it."

"A year's a long time to be sick." I made my voice curl up at the end, pointed it accusingly at the memory of our dead mother.

"Girls *didn't* then," Barclay said in a deceptively prim way he has.

"Oh no? What about Mary Morgan?"

His face squeezed into a wide smile. He remembered Mary Morgan all right, one of the old school teacher friends our mother used to talk about, Mary Morgan who was unmarried and Catholic, and who got pregnant and jumped one night off the top of a player piano in an attempt to bring about a miscarriage. For us the story of Mary Morgan's desperate leap has the sheen of legend about it, and shares space with my mother's other girlhood legends.

Brave little crippled Grace, for instance, who went to DeKalb Normal in a wheelchair, and another friend, someone called Lily, who had the habit of signing her letters, "Lovingly, Lily," one word swimming coyly beneath the other (an example is preserved in my mother's "memory book," floating loose between pressed gardenias and locks of hair).

Barclay and I were having this conversation about Mom and Mary Morgan and Grace and Lily in a downtown bar that serves good roast pork sandwiches. Barclay works as a systems engineer in Houston, and normally, when he comes to Chicago, I invite him out to the house for a family dinner. I wondered if he thought it was funny that I'd suggested we meet down in the Loop like this instead, and that I hadn't even mentioned Ray and the children. Maybe he thought I was being evasive. Probably not; he has a calm, incurious nature. He'd put on weight, I saw. Even his fingers curving around the wine glass looked puffy. What do you do for love? is the question I would like to have asked him. I imagined the words leaving my mouth and entering his soft body. No, impossible. We talked instead about our mother's friend Mary Morgan whom neither of us had ever met.

"Do you suppose it worked?" Barclay said. He meant, did she have a miscarriage, and the question surprised me. "Why, I don't know," I said with amazement.

Why didn't I know? This was an old story, after all, and I'd heard it from our mother countless times. The picture was vivid: a carved oak piano draped with some sort of fringed scarf; a woman in a flapper dress with flushed Catholic cheeks is climbing first up onto the keyboard and then onto the top of the piano itself; she crouches, then springs, and there, frozen in mid-air, she has remained. Rings of surprise surround her spread-eagled body which is weightless in flight, but determined, righteous, and stiff with terror.

"Either it worked or it didn't work," said Barclay in his committee voice. Then he said, "Maybe she died."

I said no, I didn't think so. We would have remembered that.

Neither of us could believe that our mother had told us only half the story. We agreed that we must have blocked out the ending, the moment of actual impact. "Maybe it was a nervous breakdown," Barclay said, getting back to the subject of our mother's year of illness.

This was a good possibility, and one that had also occurred to me. Our mother had been a nervous woman. Insomnia, hives, headaches, fits of harsh weeping, all the usual symptoms. "Mom's in the sadhouse again," our father would tell us from time to time. But that sad self was her later self, the self that came into being after the betrayal of her veins and the stringy deterioration of her hands. I see her as cool skinned and calm, as a young woman in her sunny Cortland schoolroom, rather like Barclay in the matter of personality.

Barclay said, "Maybe it was one of those mysterious girlish fevers women used to get. Or, what do you call it–wasting disease?"

"No one's had wasting disease since the eighteenth century," I told him.

"How about TB?"

"Impossible. She'd have gone to the San."

"Mono?" he flung out. We tried to think if people had mono in those days, it sounds so much a disease of our own generation. But no, it's an old illness; we remembered that it was once called glandular fever.

"That's a real possibility." I drummed my fingers on the dark wet table, pleased. Barclay, what a good man he was, sensed my pleasure and poured me more wine from the bubbly-sided carafe. Glandular fever. People who had glandular fever had to go to bed and stay there, perhaps as long as a year.

"Why don't you ask Auntie Ingrid?" Barclay suggested.

"I suppose I could."

"You still write back and forth, don't you?"

"Twice a year. Christmas and her birthday. I think she'd go through the floor if I just wrote to her out of the blue and asked her about a thing like that."

"Well, if you really want to know. . . ." He let his voice trail off mildly, but managed to suggest I'd been wasting his time with my speculation.

"Maybe I will," I decided. "But that's not to say I'm going to find anything out. You know how secretive our family is."

"Oh, I know that," Barclay said.

In my mother's family there were two amputations, Auntie Ingrid's finger and Uncle Harvey's leg. Even in a family with nine children this seems to me unusual.

Aunt Ingrid is my mother's twin sister; they were identical twins, the Lofgren girls from Lemond, Illinois, who looked so much alike that one of them once took a Latin test for the other without their teacher catching on. Later they liked to fool their boyfriends, my mother Anna going to the door when Ingrid's beau arrived and saying in her sly teasing voice, "I'm all ready if you are." They believed, as many twins do, that they were joined by a bond closer than mere sisterhood. In later years, Aunt Ingrid, married by then to Uncle Eugene and the mother of four children, would write from Napoleon, Indiana, where she moved, and tell my mother that she had a new perm, and it would turn out to have been on the very day my mother in Maywood gave herself a Toni. Or they would find they had had colds at the same time or bought new spring coats in the same color, or tossed and turned throughout the same restless night. More often than not their letters crossed, and this more than anything else provided proof of their joined natures.

As girls they were each other's best friend. When they were seventeen they enrolled in the teacher training course at DeKalb, traveling back and forth each day on the Interurban that ran for miles past the town limits, into the rolling countryside and stopped not far from the side road where they lived. One afternoon, arriving at their stop, my mother jumped gaily off the car, followed by Ingrid. But Ingrid was wearing a ring on her finger, a cheap ring of imitation gold, and the ring caught in the mechanism of the door. My mother remembered a strip of brown skin unwinding like a peeling off an apple. There was surprisingly little blood, but considerable confusion and shouting, and someone on the street car said loudly, "The poor girl, she's going to lose that finger."

The driver of the Interurban took Aunt Ingrid

straight back to the DeKalb hospital where she did indeed lose her finger, the fourth finger on the left, that very night.

It fell to my mother to go home and tell her parents that there had been an accident. But she did *not* tell them. She could not, she later said; her mother could not have borne it. Instead, she told them that Ingrid had gone to a friend's house in DeKalb to spend the night, and then she lay awake all night with her teeth chattering, the longest night she was ever to endure. In the morning a doctor from DeKalb drove his Model T into the farmyard, knocked at the kitchen door and informed the astonished parents that their daughter's finger had been amputated.

"I was lucky it was on the left hand," Aunt Ingrid said. "It was lucky I lost it when I was young." She graduated and became a teacher; later she married Uncle Eugene and moved to Napoleon and became a prize-winning knitter. When she wore gloves, she tucked the extra finger to the inside so that nothing showed but a neat little seam. Barclay and I as children used to ask to see her tiny knobbed stump which was pinker and harder than the rest of her hand. Did it hurt? we asked. Not a bit, she told us, not in the slightest. Now she's eighty years old and lives in a retirement center in southern California, and last year she wrote that she has begun to experience a twinge of arthritis in her stump, just a twinge, nothing serious, she says, but a reminder that a finger had once been there.

Uncle Harvey, my mother's oldest brother, lost his

leg in the war in 1916. There are no firm facts about how this loss occurred, whether it was a bullet or a bomb or what, the leg was just "lost in the war," mysteriously swallowed up in the smoking distances of Europe. He came home wounded, a man with a wooden leg and two canes to help him get around. After a few weeks of hobbling about on the farm, he took the train into Chicago and got a job as a machinery operator, and he worked at that for the rest of his life, a life that was long and alcoholic and that had a quality of deep distress about it. Whether it was the wooden leg that caused his distress I don't know, but I do know that his mother, our grandmother, was never told her son had, in fact, lost his leg. He was lame, that was all she knew. She lived until the fall of 1942, this poor deluded woman, and then she succumbed to double pneumonia, still not knowing.

My husband, Ray, who comes from a more forthcoming family, has never understood how this could have happened. Was this grandmother, this short, fat-faced woman–we have only the photographs to inform us–kept in a state of innocence because of her status as Mother, the being most closely tied to the legless man? Or was she a woman with a singular sensitivity to life's darker offerings? Would she have screamed if she'd been told? Might she have fallen into a faint or slashed her wrists or sunk into years of melancholy? Or might she have shrugged–did anyone consider this?–and said, well, that's a shame, but other boys have lost their legs and some are a lot worse off than Harvey. On one occasion the truth was almost discovered. Uncle Harvey, home for a Thanksgiving dinner, was sitting at the table lifting a turkey wing to his mouth. His mother, who was setting down a bowl of peas, put her hand on his shoulder and felt through his shirt the heavy leather strap that held the artificial leg in place. "What's this?" she said in a sharp voice.

There was a moment's awful silence. Then Uncle Harvey said, "It's for a hernia, Ma. Nothing serious."

My grandmother set down the peas and went back to the stove for the potatoes; nothing more was said. Perhaps she didn't know what a hernia was; perhaps she thought it was too delicate a subject to pursue; maybe she had her suspicions but resisted them. This, after all, was a woman who could not be told about her daughter's mutilated finger. How was she expected to bear the news of a son's lost leg? But what if suspicion gave birth to a secret, and what if the secret became part of her, like a small, benign tumor under the skin that had long since been accommodated? Turning to the stove, serving out potatoes, keeping her back turned, she may have been saying: I don't want to know, I don't want to know.

Whew, the aunts and uncles must have said afterwards; whew, that was a close call. I can imagine they made adult faces at each other over the table, mock expressions of shock and guilty amusement as though they had brushed close to something unspeakable and also foolish, something they were deeply ashamed of, but could do nothing about.

In 1925 my mother recovered from her mysterious

year of illness and came to Chicago to teach school. She and Aunt Ingrid and Mary Morgan and another girl called Gladys Heinz found an apartment on the third floor of a house in Oak Park. The house was on Kenilworth Avenue, just north of Lake Street.

And the strange part of this is that the house belonged to the Hemingway family, the parents of Ernest Hemingway.

Of course my mother had never heard of Ernest Hemingway. No one, for that matter, had really heard of him. All she knew was that the family had a son who was living in Paris, France. He was married, and his family spoke about him with a certain coolness. My mother, in her simple way, assumed that the family disapproved of their son living abroad, or else they didn't like the girl he had married. She had no idea he was a writer.

Dr. and Mrs. Hemingway interviewed the four young women on a hot, late summer day. My mother and Aunt Ingrid and Mary Morgan and Gladys Heinz all wore hats and gloves and stockings, and they sat uneasily in the airless front room, the living room, as Mrs. Hemingway called it. The Hemingways explained that they didn't normally rent out their third floor, but that their daughter, Sonny, was in college and that college was expensive. This statement was allowed to float for a minute on the still air, and then Mrs. Hemingway explained a few household rules: the rent was payable at the beginning of each month. She herself was a light sleeper and could not tolerate noise after ten o'clock. The gas bill would be shared and so would the bill for water. Baths were to be limited to two inches in the tub, which was all she herself ever required. She said that she and her husband had considered carefully the kind of people they preferred as tenants, and they both thought that young women in the teaching profession represented all that was ideal. They regretted that their son Ernest had not considered a career in education. They regretted it deeply.

The third-floor apartment contained two bedrooms and a sitting room with a shuttered-off kitchen at one end. The ceiling sloped sharply in the kitchen part of the room and, standing at the sink, they had to duck their heads, especially Mary Morgan who was taller than the others.

They took turns cooking. My mother's specialty was cheese rarebit, a soggy dish that she occasionally made for us when we were children. Aunt Ingrid made chicken à la king in toast cups. Gladys Heinz made a good nutritious meat loaf, and Mary Morgan, hopeless when it came to cooking, washed dishes night after night with her long neck bent against the ceiling.

On one occasion they were invited downstairs for Sunday dinner. There was a standing rib roast, mashed turnips, canned peas and tapioca pudding. The four of them were astonished to learn that Dr. Hemingway had done all the cooking himself. Speechless, they turned their eyes to Mrs. Hemingway who pronounced in a deep voice, "I have never taken an interest in cooking." After dessert the Hemingways talked about their children. There had been a recent letter from Sonny, but it was some time since they had heard from their son in Paris.

"Is he an artist?" Aunt Ingrid asked.

"He's a time waster," Dr. Hemingway said in a stern, settled voice.

After a brief silence my mother, anxious to prove she was *not* a time waster, said, "Can we help wash the dishes?"

"That would be useful," Mrs. Hemingway said.

Later they told each other it was all they could do to choke back their laughter. Mrs. Hemingway's stiff autocratic phrase became their private invitation to hysteria. They inverted its icy finality and made of it the signal for hilarity. If Aunt Ingrid offered to give Gladys a manicure, for instance, as she often did, Gladys would say, "That would be useful." If Mary Morgan said she was thinking of strolling down to the public library, they would all call out after her, "That would be useful." When a man named Eugene Propper proposed to Aunt Ingrid, she swore she came close to giggling out, "Why, that would be very useful."

A year later, Ernest Hemingway published *The Sun Also Rises* and became famous, but by that time my mother and Ingrid and Mary and Gladys had moved to an apartment on the west side.

This has always seemed to me to be a tragedy of timing. "Why did you move after only one year?" I used to badger my mother, and her answer was always the same: "That house was so cold, we couldn't stand it another winter. We complained and complained about the heat, but they never did a single thing about it."

My mother never read Hemingway; his reputation intimidated her, I think. I started early, at fourteen, reading him with eager pleasure, but also out of a compulsion to fulfill a side of a family contract which I felt had been allowed to lapse. It seemed to me I had been willed the sharp perspective of privilege. For instance, I would look up from certain passages in *Green Hills of Africa* and suddenly think: this is the voice of a man who grew up in an insufficiently heated house. The drafty stairs, the icy bedrooms, the two inches of bath water, all these things tore brokenly into the smoothness of his sentence parts, or so I thought, and I wanted to reach through the pages and warn him that he was in mortal danger of exposing himself. Didn't he realize what those soft places in the prose revealed? Couldn't he see what was so clearly apparent to the most casual observer, what his pathetic evasions revealed?

Lately, since I've had lots of time, I've reread his earlier books. A man I know, a man I thought I was in love with, teased me about being on a Hemingway trip, but it's really an inverse journey. I see these books differently now; what I thought were unconscious evasions, I now see as skillfully told lies, lies that have given me a new respect for Hemingway and the way he coped with a difficult life. I even started to think that perhaps I could cope with my own.

Then Aunt Ingrid's letter arrived, not a Christmas letter, not a birthday letter, but a letter that arrived in April in reply to my own unseasonable note. First she told me about the weather in San Diego, which is always superlative, and then about the complete lack of cooked vegetables at the Center. She expressed surprise at hearing from me and regretted that I hadn't sent news about Ray and the children. She assumed, though, that they were all fit and fine.

On the second page she explained that she had very little recollection about my mother's year of illness. She vaguely remembered a sickness of some kind, but was sure it was of shorter duration, six weeks at the most. She suggested influenza and then, as an afterthought, eyestrain. She went on to say, "I can't for the life of me see why you want to delve into all this ancient history."

The tone was rough, cross; she meant to put me in my place and she did. I couldn't really blame her. Lies, secrets, casual misrepresentations and small failures of memory, all these things are useful in their way. History gobbles everything up willy-nilly; it doesn't care a fig for distinctions; it was all the same. My mother's illness has the same weight as a missing finger or a wooden leg or a fizzled-out love affair. Eventually, everything gets stuck between a pair of parentheses or buried in the bottom of a trunk.

I was thinking about this when the phone rang. It was my husband Ray suggesting we have dinner together. Why not? I said. We met at a place on Rush Street known for its good authentic Basque food, and afterward we sat talking for an hour or two.

He told me the saddest thing that had ever happened to him was seeing the movie *Easy Rider*, and then coming home and climbing into a pair of striped pajamas and going to bed. I asked him why he'd never told me this before, and he said he didn't know. I accused him of being secretive, and he smiled and said he'd probably learned it from me.

I started to tell him the saddest thing in my life was the bundle of worthless secrets I carry around in my head, but then I smiled back at him and said that I loved my secrets, that I would be lost without them, that they were the only things in the world I could call my own.

Fuel for the Fire

When you think about holidays like Thanksgiving and Christmas and Easter, and those huge traditional dinners with roast meat and bowls of mashed potatoes and fruit pies laid out, you tend to imagine city families wrapping up in their warm coats and climbing into cars and driving out to the family farm. That's the way it was with us, but no longer. Now, since Mom died three years ago, my dad comes into Winnipeg for those special days. He drives the pickup, not the Pontiac. He's used to it, he says. It hugs the road better, and it seems there's always something or other he needs to haul. As a matter of fact, he's here most Sundays too. It's only forty-five miles, and he's careful to pick a time when the highway's relatively quiet.

He's never been the world's best driver. Not that

he's ever had a real accident, but traffic makes him nervous. He gets heart palpitations, so he says. He's okay on secondary roads, and around McLeod, but not in the city. When Mom was still in good health he always tried to wheedle her into taking the wheel when they went to Portage to shop. We used to kill ourselves laughing about that, the traffic in Portage la Prairie. But now he sails into Winnipeg almost every week. He comes in on the Number 1 Highway, takes a left at Silversides Boulevard, another left at Union, and then a sharp right into our driveway.

I always give him a cup of coffee the minute he gets here. Or, if it's lunch time, a bowl of soup. He can sink down a pan of soup just like that, cream of chicken or asparagus, if I've got it on hand. Campbell's asparagus, that's his idea of real gourmet. He doesn't mind trying new things, even lasagna or beef curry. I read an article not long ago about how old people's taste buds shrivel up with age so that they actually need more spice in their food, not less. When I told him we were having goose for New Year's Day dinner, he looked really interested. He's never had goose before. Neither have I for that matter. Neither has Dennis.

But we're all sick of turkey. We had turkey last week for Christmas, and a pork loin for Boxing Day, and I know Dad wouldn't touch lamb. So what's left? There aren't all that many edible animals when you think about it. Which is why I decided to try a goose this year, a ten-pounder. I ordered it special from DeLuca's downtown, and if Dad knew what I paid for this hunk of bird he'd have a conniption. If he asks me outright, as he's apt to do, I plan to start humming loudly or put the radio on.

It's early morning, only eight o'clock, when I get
out of bed on New Year's Day. Dennis and I were out
at our annual potluck last night, just four couples,
the same bunch every year, and didn't get home till
three-thirty–but I don't need all that much sleep.
Today a dozen sirens kicked me awake. First, I forgot
to take the goose out of the deep-freeze yesterday,
and now I'm having to fast-thaw it in a sinkful of
warm water, poking my arm way up into its icy
ribcage. Its skin looks bluish-gray and very prickly
around the thighs, not especially appealing. Then
there's the stuffing to make. I'm trying out a new
mushroom and cashew recipe, and I'm also going to
serve a squash soufflé with green onions and
chopped parsley for color. I put chopped parsley on
everything; it's got lots of iron. When Dennis and I
were first married, he used to give me a hard time
about my chopped parsley and said I'd probably
sprinkle a handful on his dead corpse if he went first.
Now he's used to it; he's actually got so he likes it.

He's still asleep, Dennis. I always get up first on
holidays, there's so much to do. Besides the stuffing
and the squash thing, I want to mop the kitchen floor
and clean out the fireplace. I like to have things
organized before the kids get too wound up and
before Dennis starts thinking up projects. He'll want
to take the tree down, I know that, but I want it up
one more day. I'd just as soon take it down myself
tomorrow when he's gone back to work and the kids
are back at school.

There are going to be eight of us for dinner. Besides
Dad and Dennis and the three kids and myself, I've
invited Sally and Purse from next door. They're older
than we are, just halfway in age between Dad's

seventy-five and my thirty-four, and their two kids have grown up and moved east. Purse is a commodities dealer, oil seeds mainly, and Sally's been selling real estate for the last eight years. She's good at it. She's already made it into the Million Dollar Club. She had her membership key imbedded in a silver disc and wears it like a brooch on the lapel of her coat. Dad gets a kick out of her. He really likes to get her going, and she eggs him on. He can't believe the prices of houses in Winnipeg, what people will pay for jerry-built construction and hanky-sized lots. Last week, never mind the slow December market, Sally sold a house in Tuxedo for half a million dollars, and it didn't even have a full basement. The heating bills for this particular house are more than Dennis and I pay every month for our mortgage and taxes combined, but then our heating bills are pretty high too. Like everyone else around here, we switched from oil to gas a few years ago. This is a cold climate. You've got to put out a lot of your income on heat in this part of the country, but every night, from September to May, we have a fire in our fireplace, and I like to think that that takes some of the burden off the furnace.

Most of our friends who have fireplaces use them maybe three or four times a year. Cordwood's expensive, they say, but then they admit it's really the mess and bother of cleaning out the ashes. I do it fast first thing in the morning, a little whisk broom and dustpan and a metal pail for the ashes. I can clean our fireplace in three minutes flat, I've timed myself. The ashes I save to put on the garden in the springtime.

I love a fire. I'm addicted, we both are, but

especially me. I get the kids to bed at night and, by the time I come downstairs, Dennis has a fair blaze going. We got into the fire habit when he was doing his graduate work in England (genetics, swine). We had a little rented house there, two rooms up, two rooms down. We didn't have a TV, we couldn't afford a baby sitter, but we had this real fireplace. Of course it wasn't a luxury there, it was how we heated the house more or less. But neither of us had grown up with a fireplace. It was something new. It was company, like a person, like our best friend. We made toast in it sometimes for a bedtime snack and, if I happened to have any orange peels left over, I'd throw them in and wait for the orange smell to fill up the room. We burned pinecones, too, if we found any, and once I remember we put in one of those padded book envelopes and watched the little plastic pillows of air explode in the heat. It was only a year and a half we were there, but it seemed to stretch out much longer, sitting in front of that fireplace with the radio on low and reading library books. We hadn't counted on this, it was a surprise. It was like living in a dark crack, just the two of us keeping warm in our own dust, and Danny sleeping in his crib upstairs.

Back home we borrowed money from my folks and started looking around for a house of our own. The one thing I wanted most was a fireplace. It was at the top of the list. I pretty well knew by then that being content had to do with crackling flames and baked shins. I didn't care about a garage or a family room or whether there was four inches of insulation in the roof, as long as we had something hot and alive to sit around at night, keeping *us* alive.

Our Winnipeg fireplace is painted-over brick, off-white to match the living-room walls, with a rounded opening like one of those old-fashioned bread ovens. It draws like a dream and it's got a damper we can open and close, which is very important in our climate. Next to it is a brass stand for the fireplace implements, and next to that is a woven brass basket holding birch logs. The birch logs are just for show; at the moment we're burning scrap lumber Dad hauled in from the farm.

He's crazy about our fireplace. He says he sees all kinds of pictures in the flames, a hundred times better than anything on TV. For a while he even tried to talk Mom into getting one installed at the farm. She wasn't too fussy about the idea, not after all those years she spent dealing with a cookstove, but she told him to go ahead if he had his mind made up. In the end he decided it was too much money. According to Sally, it costs about six thousand to install a fireplace after construction, but adds only fifteen hundred dollars to the value of a house.

In her old age my mother shrank down to nothing. Her feet ached all the time. She stopped driving the car, she stopped cooking. She got little fruity eyes and a dented chin. I hardly recognized her. She refused to go out of the house in wintertime, even to Portage. She didn't want to miss her shows, she said. She and the TV and the living-room rad were like a little unbreakable triangle. She wore a pair of wool and angora socks that came up over her knees, and a thick cardigan, and always had an afghan at hand. She hardly talked to us toward the end, she was so occupied with keeping warm and staying off her feet.

It scared me seeing her like that, which is why, more or less, I signed up for the refresher course at the hospital this year with the idea of maybe going back to work part-time when Tom starts Grade One.

By midmorning I have the table set in the dining ell. I'm using Mom's old damask tablecloth today, which is murder to iron but shines flat like ice under my good tulip china. But not the damask napkins, not with three kids and a goose that looks like it's got a lot of bluish fat on it. I've splurged on big thick paper napkins in a soft shade of rose, also six pale pink candles for my crystal candlesticks. Knowing Sally and Purse, we'll have pink flowers on the table too, and Lara, our nine-year-old, will want to make place cards. I'll tell her to do them on white cardboard with a pink felt-tipped pen.

Dennis is a little crabby when he gets up. He watches me pile mushroom stuffing into the goose's insides and says, "You sure that's going to be big enough to go around."

"It's supposed to serve twelve," I tell him, and I think again how much I paid for it. The thought just washes over me for a minute, all that money, what we used to spend on food in a whole week.

"Hmmmmm," he says, his skeptical voice which I don't really appreciate. I ask him to carry some firewood up from the basement for tonight. Yes, yes, he says automatically, but he stands there drinking coffee and just looking at me.

Last summer my dad demolished an old shed in back of his barn. We don't know why he took it down. Dennis thinks he was just trying to keep himself busy. He doesn't actually farm anymore, but he lives in the old house and rents out the acreage.

I've tried to talk him into moving to Winnipeg, and Sally even took him to view some basement suites not far from here. For a while he seemed interested. We tried to impress on him that he could walk over here and have dinner with us at night and see a lot more of the kids as they grew up. But I think he worried about what he'd do all day in a dinky basement suite. He's a very, very sociable man. Every morning, for as long as I can remember, he's driven the half mile into McLeod for coffee and toast at the McLeod Luncheonette. He'll generally sit there for an hour, shooting the breeze. There are five or six of them, all farmers from around the area. He'd miss that. Sally finally took me aside and said she didn't think it was such a great idea, his moving to Winnipeg. She doesn't think he's ready. Maybe later on, she says, when he's less self-sufficient.

Besides being sociable, he's extremely active physically. Taking down that shed was hard work. You have to be methodical taking down a building, more so than putting one up, especially working on your own. You have to pay attention or the whole thing can come crashing down on your head. It took him about a week, and at the end of the week he drove into Winnipeg and delivered the first of several truckloads of two-by-fours and other assorted bits of wood. "You might as well make use of this," he said. "In the fireplace."

It wasn't that big a shed as I remember, but somehow we've ended up with this basement full of ugly lumber. Dennis says it's going to last us forever. The boards are full of nails and, when I clean out the ashes in the mornings, I have to gather up the blackened nails too. Some of them get stuck in the grate and it's a real job prying them out. But, on the other hand, there's not much point in buying firewood when we've got all this scrap wood to use up. It isn't as though we're heating the house with the fireplace, as Dad says. It's just for enjoyment. He can't believe that people actually go into supermarkets and buy Prestologs. Prestologs floor him completely, the whole idea of manufacturing something for the purpose of burning it up.

Around noon I give Dennis and the kids a pick-up lunch, and while we sit talking at the kitchen table I look up and see Dad passing by the window. We never even heard him drive up. He smiles at us through the frosted glass, and I can see how we must look to him with our grilled cheese and glasses of milk and talk. The shoulders of his big plaid jacket are stippled with snow and his eyes seem vague as though the pupils are only parked there temporarily. "Is that goose I'm smelling?" he asks, coming in through the back way. I say yes, that I put it in the oven an hour ago. He looks happy, anticipatory.

In the afternoon, while the goose spits and crackles in the roasting pan, Dennis takes Dad to the New Year's Day Levee at the Legislative Building. This happens here every New Year's Day. In the old days it was a military affair, a strictly male-only event, but now the general public is invited, even kids. For entertainment there's an RCMP band and a troop of Scotch pipers in full regalia. You line up and shake hands with the premier of Manitoba and his wife, the lieutenant governor and *his* wife, and then you have a glass of Gimli Goose, which is a kind of pinkish wine, and some fruitcake or shortbread.

Our two older kids look as though they wouldn't

mind going along, but I like the idea of Dennis and
Dad being off on their own for a change. Dennis's
folks live down in Nova Scotia, and they're not the
sort that gets together anyway. A few times Dennis
has tried taking Dad to hockey games, but it's not
easy for an older man sitting so long on those hard
seats. He always looks forward to the New Year's
Levee. Today he's brought along his suit on a hanger
and his white shirt and tie. He changes just before
they set off, and on the way they drop the kids off at
the rink.

The afternoon is slow and dozy, and the sun
pouring in through the front window makes me feel
sleepy. I settle down on the chesterfield and read an
article in the paper about the right kind of clothes to
wear for job interviews. I've read this same kind of
article a thousand times, but I still need to read it,
something makes me. Not too much jewelry. No
sandals. A well-made suit in a neutral tone is still the
best bet, with a muted scarf for a feminine touch.
That's as far as I get before dropping off to sleep.

I can't have slept for long, maybe three-quarters of
an hour, but when I wake up I sniff the air for the
smell of goose and don't smell anything. I head
straight for the kitchen, and sure enough the oven's
barely warm. So down I go to the basement to check
the fuses, but they're all in order. Then I put on my
oven mitts and jiggle the element at the bottom of the
oven, in case it's worked its way loose. A corner of it
looks black and slightly shriveled. This happened
once or twice before, a burnt-out element, but not on
a holiday, and not when I was cooking an expensive
goose.

My first idea is to carry the roasting pan over to

Sally's and finish it off in her oven, but then I remember that she and Purse are out for the afternoon. And all the other people around here are using their ovens for *their* holiday dinners. I consider what would happen to the poor old thing if I tried cooking it very slowly on top of the stove, maybe pouring a little wine around to keep it from burning. It would probably get rubbery, or else stringy. Boiled goose doesn't sound like much of a dish. But at that moment, luckily, Dennis and Dad come through the back door.

They take off their coats and go straight to work. First Dennis takes the goose out and wraps it up with foil to try to preserve what little heat is left. Then he and Dad pull the stove away from the wall, disconnect it, and start examining the bolts that hold the element in place. Definitely burnt out, Dennis says, sounding not one bit dismayed, not an iota, just the opposite.

From the basement he carries up a set of screwdrivers and wrenches, as well as his soldering gear. Before buckling down to work, he pours Dad a tall rye and ginger ale, a heart-starter he calls it, and one for himself. He's humming away and concentrating hard as he slips his wrench around the first of the bolts.

I pull up the aluminum foil for a peek at my goose. It looks pale and glum with its dead meaty chest cooling down fast. I remember the time Dennis and I went to the British Museum to look at the mummies, how depressed I was to find just how dead you could actually get, but Dennis was all over the room, peering at everything and snapping photographs, though, strictly speaking, this wasn't allowed.

He'll have the stove working in less than an hour, he tells me. He doesn't even stop to think about what he's going to do. It's as though he's got a pocket of his brain filled with little mechanical puzzles that he can undo at will. He's going to remove the burnt-out unit and move the broiler element temporarily down to the bottom of the oven. An emergency tactic. He's whistling now. Unlike me, he appreciates the unexpected. Dad is handing him tools in a rhythmic nurse-to-surgeon manner and trying hard, I can tell, to bite his tongue and keep from giving Dennis advice. It's hard for him not being in full charge. He's a sweetheart, but pig-headed at times.

Right after Mom died–I'm talking about one month after she went–Dad cut down all the lilac bushes around their house. These lilacs were old, more like trees than bushes. They'd always been there, protecting the house from the wind and the open stare of the road. He claimed he and Mom had often talked about chopping them down so they could get more sunshine into the house. I have my doubts about this–my mother loved those lilacs– but we let the story stand.

He cut the twisted old lilac wood into short lengths and bundled them up for our fireplace. Good for kindling, he said. And he also hauled the roots, sixteen of them, into town. First he shook off as much dirt as he could. Lilac roots are dense, damp, shrubby things, irregular in shape and amazingly large. I think he was surprised himself at the size of them.

They burned very slowly. A single lilac root takes a whole evening to burn. You have to poke it continually to keep it going, and it smolders rather than flames. Now and then it gives a turquoise colour, just a flash. There's no smell of lilac at all, but from time to time the whole root takes on a sort of glow, shadowy and three-dimensional like a human face burning, eyes and mouth and wrinkled cheeks all lit up and keeping itself intact right to the point of disintegration. We still talk about it, Dad and his lilac roots. Even the children remember, or say they can.

By five o'clock the goose is back in the oven, sputtering fat and getting golden. And by seven o'clock the eight of us are seated at the table. Our faces look coral. Dennis carves, looking not quite at me, across the table. Dad carefully tastes a bit of goose, then says, as if he's looking a long way back into the past, "It reminds me a bit of pheasant, only meatier." Sally runs through her recent Tuxedo triumph and Purse shares his nice rambling educated laugh around the table. We go counter-clockwise, telling our New Year's resolutions. Dad says he's going to think seriously about a trip to Florida, which I'll believe when I see it. Sally's signed up for calligraphy. Purse is giving up white sugar. The kids look giggly and secretive and won't say, even when I prod them. Dennis announces his resolution to run the mini-marathon in April. He says this in a staunch, wilful, but kindly way. I'm going to master the art of crepe making, I say, but my real resolve, the one I don't mention, is to stop managing everyone's lives for them.

After dessert the three men insist on doing dishes. Sally and I sit in the living room waiting for them. The waiting seems like a treasure we've piled up, something we owe ourselves. We settle back into soft cushions and put up our feet in front of the fireplace. But then I remember I've forgotten to lay a fire. And what with the goose crisis, Dennis has forgotten to bring up any firewood. We look at each other, at the birch logs sitting there, and say, why not?

"Hold on a sec," Dad says, coming in from the kitchen. "I'll be right back." He puts on his coat and boots and five minutes later he's back with a large carton of bowling pins.

The bowling alley in McLeod's been shut down for years, just like the old McLeod movie theater and the old high school and just about everything else. A lot of the small central region towns are shrinking away to nothing, and McLeod suffers particularly by being just a little too close to Portage. The old buildings were boarded up ages ago, but somewhere Dad heard about the stockpile of bowling pins sitting there going to waste in the abandoned bowling alley.

A signal must have registered in his head, a dotted line stretching from the old bowling lanes direct to our fireplace. Other people might see something nostalgic or sad, but he took a look and saw fuel. Bowling pins are wood. They're burnable.

It never before occurred to me to wonder what a bowling pin might look like on the inside, but I would have guessed they were solid through and through, cut with a lathe out of chunks of tough dry hardwood. But they're not. They're glued together in two lengthwise sections, and there's a little hollow–oval shaped–in the middle.

They take a while to catch alight. You need lots of kindling, little chips of hardwood or balled-up newspaper. Then you see a flare of white light, which is the paint catching fire (the pins are painted an ivory color with a red stripe around their middles), and before you know it the entire skin is flaky ash. Then the fire finds a way into the core. The center burns brightly, deeply red, so that the sides look transparent, more like glass than wood, more like bottles than bowling pins. The red heart keeps getting brighter and brighter and then, suddenly, with a snap it cracks open. "Thar she blows," Sally says, seconds before the third pin splits itself exactly in two.

Dennis leans over and gently places two more nose to nose on the grate. He's loving this. By now we've turned out the floor lamp and all the table lamps, leaving just the lit tree and the light from the fire.

It makes me dizzy looking at those pins burning. I think, now they're going, now they're gone. I remember the last time Dennis and I were on a plane, and the pilot, crossing a time zone, asked us to adjust our time pieces. Our time pieces. What a word. We twiddled a dial, and there was an hour erased.

Purse is talking about growing up in Swan River, how he used to set pins after school, earning thirty cents an hour and how he read *True Detective Magazine* between lanes. The kids stare at his face, which happens to be a rather large, quiet, undemanding face, and I can tell they're wondering how things get so displaced and changed like this.

I look over at Dad who's asleep in his chair. It's been a longer day than he's used to, and I'm glad he's decided to sleep over. There's pink light from the fire coloring up his forehead and cheeks. It's extravagant looking, rich, and I can't decide whether it makes him look very old or young like a boy.

Sally sits close to me. Earlier, while the men were

doing the dishes and the kids were tearing around the house, I told her I was thinking of going back to work as soon as possible, not waiting till next fall after all. She listened hard. She has a lot of strong curiosity about her. "Don't rush," she said. "Work is only work."

"One more?" Dennis asks us, and balances another pin delicately on its side in the glowing ashes. It flares, catches, glows, splits open and dies. I pay attention to it. Usually I'm so preoccupied, so busy, I forget about this odd ability of time to overtake us. Then something reminds me. Cemeteries–they stop me short, do they *ever* stop me short–and old buildings and tree stumps, things like that. And the sight of burning fires, like tonight, like right now, this minute, how economical it is, how it eats up everything we give it, everything we have to offer.

Milk Bread Beer Ice

"What's the difference between a gully and a gulch?" Barbara Cormin asks her husband, Peter Cormin, as they speed south on the Interstate. These are the first words to pass between them in over an hour, this laconic, idle, unhopefully offered, trivia-contoured question.

Peter Cormin, driving a cautious sixty miles an hour through a drizzle of rain, makes no reply, and Barbara, from long experience, expects none. Her question concerning the difference between gullies and gulches floats out of her mouth like a smoker's lazy exhalation and is instantly subsumed by the hum of the engine. Two minutes pass. Five minutes. Barbara's thoughts skip to different geological features, the curious wind-lashed forms she sees through the car window, and those others whose names she vaguely remembers from a compulsory geology course taken years earlier–arroyos, cirques, terminal moraines. She has no idea now what these exotic relics might look like, but imagines them to be so brutal and arresting as to be instantly recognizable should they materialize on the landscape. Please let them materialize, she prays to the grooved door of the glove compartment. Let something, *anything*, materialize.

This is their fifth day on the road. Four motels, interchangeable, with tawny, fire-retardant carpeting, are all that have intervened. This morning, Day Five, they drive through a strong brown and yellow landscape, ferociously eroded, and it cheers Barbara a little to gaze out at this scene of novelty after seventeen hundred miles of green hills and ponds and calm, staring cattle. "I really should keep a dictionary in the car," she says to Peter, another languid exhalation.

The car, with its new car smell, seems to hold both complaint and accord this morning. And silence. Barbara sits looking out at the rain, wondering about the origin of the word drizzle–a likeable enough word, she thinks, when you aren't actually being drizzled upon. Probably onomatopoetic. Drizzling clouds. Drizzled syrup on pancakes. She thrashes around in her head for the French equivalent: *bruine*, she thinks, or is that the word for fog? "I hate not knowing things," she says aloud to Peter. Musing. And arranging her body for the next five minutes.

At age fifty-three she is a restless traveler, forever shifting from haunch to haunch, tugging her blue cotton skirt smooth, examining its weave, sighing and stretching and fiddling in a disapproving way with the car radio. All she gets is country music. Or shouting call-in shows, heavy with sarcasm and whining indignation. Or nasal evangelists. Yesterday she and Peter listened briefly to someone preaching about the seven F's of Christian love, the first F being, to her amazement, the fear of God, the *feah of Gawd*. Today, because of the rain, there's nothing on the radio but ratchety static. She and Peter have brought along a box of tapes, Bach and Handel and Vivaldi, that she methodically plays and replays, always expecting diversion and always forgetting she is someone who doesn't know what to do with music. She listens but doesn't hear. What she likes are words. *Drizzle*, she repeats to herself, *bruiner*. But how to conjugate it?

In the back seat are her maps and travel guides, a bundle of slippery brochures, a book called *Place Names of Texas* and another called *Texas Wildlife*. Her reference shelf. Her sanity cupboard. She can't remember how she acquired the habit of looking up facts; out of some nursery certitude, probably, connecting virtue with an active, inquiring mind. *People must never stop learning*; once Barbara had believed fervently in this embarrassing cliché, was the first in line for night-school classes, tuned in regularly with perhaps a dozen others to solemn radio talks on existentialism, Monday nights, seven to eight. And she has, too, her weekly French conversation group, now in its fourteenth year but soon to disband.

Her brain is always heating up; inappropriately, whimsically. She rather despises herself for it, and wishes, when she goes on vacation, that she could submerge herself in scenery or fantasy as other people seemed to do, her husband Peter in particular, or so she suspects. She would never risk saying to him, "A penny for your thoughts," nor would he ever say such a thing to her. He believes such "openers" are ill-bred intrusions. He told her as much, soon after they were married, lying above her on the living-room floor in their first apartment with the oval braided rug beneath them pushing up its rounded cushiony ribs. "What are you thinking?" she had asked, and watched his eyes go cold.

The rain increases, little checks against the car window, and Barbara curls her legs up under her, something she seldom does–since it makes her feel like a woman trying too hard to be whimsical–and busies herself looking up Waco, Texas, in her guide-book. There it is: population figures, rainfall statistics, a naive but jaunty potted history. Why at her age does she feel compelled to know such things? What is all this shrewdness working itself up for? Waco, she learns, is pronounced with a long A sound, which is disappointing. She prefers–who wouldn't?–the comic splat of wham, pow, whacko. Waco, Texas. The city rises and collapses in the rainy distance.

Leaning forward, she changes the tape. Its absolute, neat plastic corners remind her of the nature of real things, and snapping it into place gives her more satisfaction than listening to the music. A click, a short silence, and then the violins stirring themselves like iced-tea spoons, like ferns on a breezy hillside. Side two. She stares out the window, watchful for the least variation. A water tower holds her eye for a full sixty seconds, a silver thimble on stilts. *Château d'eau*, she murmurs to herself. Tower of Water. Tower of Babel.

Almost all her conversations are with herself.

Imprisoned now for five long days in the passenger seat of a brand new Oldsmobile Cutlass, Barbara thinks of herself as a castaway. Her real life has been left behind in Toronto. She and Peter are en route to Houston to attend an estate auction of a late client of Peter's, a man who ended his life not long ago with a pistol shot. For the sake of the passage, admittedly only two weeks, she has surrendered those routines that make her feel busy and purposeful. (With another woman she runs an establishment on Queen Street called the Ungift Shop; she also reads to the blind and keeps up her French.) Given the confining nature of her life, she has surprising freedoms at her disposal.

We should have flown is the phrase she is constantly on the point of uttering. Driving had been Peter's idea; she can't now remember his reasons; two reasons he gave, but what were they?

He has a craning look when he drives, immensely responsible. And a way of signaling when he passes, letting his thumb wing out sideways on the lever, a deft and lovely motion. She is struck by the beauty of it, also its absurdity, a little dwarfish, unconscious salute, and silent.

There is too much sorrowful sharing in marriage, Barbara thinks. When added up, it kills words. Games have to be invented; theater. Out loud she says, like an imitation of a gawking person, "I wonder what those little red flowers are." (Turning, reaching for her wildlife book.) "We don't have those in Ontario. Or do we?"

The mention of the red flowers comes after another long silence.

Then Peter says, not unkindly, not even impatiently, "A gully's deeper, I think."

"Deeper?" says Barbara in her dream voice. She is straining her eyes to read a billboard poised high on a yellow bluff. IF YOU SMOKE PLEASE TRY CARLETONS. The word *please*, it's shocking. So!–the tobacco industry has decided to get polite. Backed into a corner, attacked on all sides, they're hitting hard with wheedling courtesies, *please*. Last week Barbara watched a TV documentary on lung cancer and saw a set of succulent pink lungs turning into what looked like slices of burnt toast.

"Deeper than a gulch."

"Oh," says Barbara.

"Unless I've got it the wrong way round."

"It's slang anyway, I think."

"What?"

"Gully. Gulch. They're not real words, are they? They sound, you know, regional. Cowboy lingo."

Peter takes a long banked curve. On and on it goes, ninety degrees or more, but finely graded. His hands on the wheel are scarcely required to move. Clean, thick hands, they might be carved out of twin bars of soap. Ivory soap, carbolic. He smiles faintly, but in a way that shuts Barbara out. On and on. Rain falls all around them–*il pleut*–on the windshield and on the twisted landforms and collecting along the roadway in ditches. "Could be," Peter says.

"Does that look brighter up ahead to you?" Barbara says wildly, anxious now to keep the conversation going. She puts away the tape, sits up straight, pats her hair, and readies herself for the little fates and accidents a conversation can provide.

Conservation?

Inside her head a quizzing eyebrow shoots up. These idle questions and observations? This dilatory response? This disobliging exchange between herself and her husband of thirty-three years, which is as random and broken as the geological rubble she dully observes from the car window, and about which Peter can scarcely trouble himself to comment? This sludge of gummed phrases? Conversation?

It could be worse, thinks Barbara, always anxious to be fair, and calling to mind real and imaginary couples sitting silent in coffee shops, whole meals consumed and paid for with not a single word exchanged. Or stunned looking husbands and wives at home in their vacuumed living rooms, neatly dressed and conquered utterly by the background hum of furnaces and air-conditioning units. And after that, what?–a desperate slide into hippo grunts and night coughing, slack, sponge-soft lips and toothless dread–that word *mute* multiplied to the thousandth power. Death.

An opportunity to break in the new car was what Peter had said–now she remembered.

Barbara met Peter in 1955 at a silver auction in Quebec City. He was an apprentice then, learning the business. He struck her first as being very quiet. He stared and stared at an antique coffee service, either assessing its value or awestruck by its beauty–she didn't know which. Later he grew talkative. Then silent. Then eloquent. Secretive. Verbose. Introspective. Gregarious. A whole colony of choices appeared to rest in his larynx. She never knew what to expect. One minute they were on trustworthy ground, feeding each other intimacies, and the next minute they were capsized, adrift and dumb.

"Some things can't be put into words," a leaner, nervous, younger Peter Cormin once said.

"Marriage can be defined as a lifelong conversation," said an elderly, sentimental, slightly literary aunt of Barbara's, meaning to be kind.

Barbara at twenty had felt the chill press of rhetorical echo: *a religious vocation is one of continuous prayer, a human life is one unbroken thought*. Frightening. She knew better, though, than to trust what was cogently expressed. Even as a young woman she was forever tripping over abandoned proverbs. She counted on nothing, but hoped for everything.

Breaking in the new car. But did people still break in cars? She hadn't heard the term used for years. Donkey's years. Whatever that meant.

A younger, thinner, more devious Barbara put planning into her conversations. There was breakfast talk and dinner talk and lively hurried telephone chatter in between. She often cast herself in the role of ingénue, allowing her husband Peter space for commentary and suggestions. It was Barbara who put her head to one side, posed questions and prettily waited. It was part of their early shared mythology that he was sometimes arrogant to the point of unkindness, and that she was sensitive and put upon, an injured consciousness flayed by husbandly imperative. But neither of them had the ability to sustain their roles for long.

She learned certain tricks of subversions, how with one word or phrase she could bring about disorder and then reassurance. It excited her. It was like flying in a flimsy aircraft and looking at the suddenly vertical horizon, then bringing everything level once more.

"You've changed," one of her conversations began.

"Everyone changes."

"For better or worse?"

"Better, I think."

"You think?"

"I know."

"You say things differently. You intellectualize."

"Maybe that's my nature."

"It didn't used to be."

"I've changed, people do change."

"That's just what I said."

"I wish you wouldn't–"

"What?"

"Point things out. Do you always have to point things out?"

"I can't help it."

"You could stop yourself."

"That wouldn't be me."

Once they went to a restaurant to celebrate the birth of their second son. The restaurant was inexpensive and the food only moderately good. After coffee, after glasses of recklessly ordered brandy, Peter slipped away to the telephone. A business call, he said to Barbara. He would only be a minute or two. From where she sat she could see him behind the glass door of the phone booth, his uplifted arm, his patient explanation, and his glance at his watch–then his face reshaped itself into furrows of explosive laughter.

She had been filled with a comradely envy for his momentary connection, and surprised by her lack of curiosity, how little she cared who was on the other end of the line, a client or a lover, it didn't matter. A conversation was in progress. Words were being mainlined straight into Peter's ear, and the overflow of his conversation traveled across the dull white tablecloths and reached her too, filling her emptiness, or part of it.

Between the two of them they have accumulated a minor treasury of anecdotes beginning with "Remember when we–" and this literature of remembrance sometimes traps them into smugness. And, occasionally, when primed by a solid period of calm, they are propelled into the blue-tinged pre-history of that epoch before they met.

"When I was in Denver that time–"

"I never knew you were in Denver."

"My mother took me there once. . . ."

"You never told me your mother took you to. . . ."

But Barbara is tenderly protective of her beginnings. She is also, oddly, protective of Peter's. Eruptions from this particular and most cherished layer of time are precious and dangerous; retrieval betrays it, smudges it.

"There's something wrong," Barbara said to Peter some years ago, "and I don't know how to tell you."

They were standing in a public garden near their house, walking between beds of tulips.

"You don't love me," he guessed, amazing her, and himself.

"I love you but not enough."

"What is enough?" he cried and reached out for the cotton sleeve of her dress.

A marriage counselor booked them for twelve sessions. Each session lasted two hours, twenty-four hours in all. During those twenty-four hours they released into the mild air of the marriage counselor's office millions of words. Their longest conversation. The polished floor, the walls, the perforated ceiling tile drank in the unstoppable flow. Barbara Cormin wept and shouted. Peter Cormin moaned, retreated, put his head on his arms. The histories they separately recounted were as detailed as the thick soft novels people carry with them to the beach in the summer. Every story elicited a counter story, until the accumulated weight of blame and blemish had squeezed them dry. "What are we doing?" Peter Cormin said, moving the back of his hand across and across his mouth. Barbara thought back to the day she had stood by the sunlit tulip bed and said, "Something's wrong," and wondered now what had possessed her. A hunger for words, was that all? She asked the marriage counselor for a glass of cold water. She feared what lay ahead. A long fall into silence. An expensive drowning.

But they were surprisingly happy for quite some time after, speaking to each other kindly, with a highly specific strategy, little pieces moved on a chess board. What had been tricky territory before was strewn with shame. Barbara was prepared now to admit that marriage was, at best, a flawed and gappy narrative. Occasionally some confidence would wobble forward and, one of them, Barbara or Peter, might look up cunningly, ready to measure the moment and retreat or advance. They worked around the reserves of each other's inattention the way a pen and ink artist learns to use the reserve of white space.

"Why?" Barbara asked Peter.

"Why what?"

"Why did he do it? Shoot himself."

"No one knows for sure."

"There's always a note. Wasn't there a note?"

"Yes. But very short."

"Saying?"

"He was lonely."

"That's what he said, that he was lonely?"

"More or less."

"What exactly did he say?"

"That there was no one he could talk to."

"He had a family, didn't he? And business associates. He had you, he's known you for years. He could have picked up the phone."

"Talking isn't just words."

"What?"

Barbara sees herself as someone always waiting for the next conversation, the way a drunk is forever thinking ahead to the next drink.

But she discounts the conversation of Eros which seems to her to be learned not from life, but from films or trashy novels whose authors have in turn learned it from other secondary and substandard sources. Where bodies collide most gloriously, language melts–who said that? Someone or other. Barbara imagines that listening at the bedroom keyholes of even the most richly articulate would be to hear only the murmurous inanities of *True Romance*. ("I adore your golden breasts," he whispered gruffly. "You give me intense pleasure," she deeply sighed.) But these conversations actually take place. She knows they do. The words are pronounced. The sighing and whispering happen. *Just the two of us, this paradise.*

"We can break in the car," Peter said to her back in Toronto, "and have a few days together, just the two of us."

Very late on Day Five they leave the Interstate and strike off on a narrow asphalt road in search of a motel. The cessation of highway noise is stunningly sudden, like swimming away in a dream from the noises of one's own body. Peter holds his head to one side, judging the car's performance, the motor's renewed, slower throb and the faint adhesive tick of the tires rolling on the hot road.

The towns they pass through are poor, but have seen better days. Sidewalks leading up to lovely old houses have crumbled along their edges, and the houses themselves have begun to deteriorate; many are for sale; dark shaggy cottonwoods bend down their branches to meet the graceful pitch of the roofs. Everywhere in these little towns there are boarded-up railway stations, high schools, laundries, cafés, plumbing supply stores, filling stations. And almost everywhere, it seems, the commercial center has shrunk to a single, blinking, all-purpose, twenty-four-hour outlet at the end of town–pathetically, but precisely named: the Mini-Mart, the Superette, the Quik-Stop. These new buildings are of single-story slab construction in pale brick or cement block, and are minimally landscaped. One or two gas pumps sit out in front, and above them is a sign, most often homemade, saying MILK ICE BREAD BEER.

"Milk ice bread beer," murmurs the exhausted Barbara, giving the phrase a heaving tune. She is diverted by the thought of these four purposeful commodities traded to a diminished and deprived public. "The four elements."

In the very next town, up and down over a series of dark hills, they find a subtly altered version: BEER ICE BREAD MILK. "Priorities," says Peter, reading the sign aloud, making an ironic chant of it.

Further along the road they come upon BREAD BEER MILK ICE. Later still, the rescrambled BEER MILK ICE BREAD.

Before they arrive, finally, at a motel with air conditioning, a restaurant and decent beds–no easy matter in a depressed agricultural region–they have seen many such signs and in all possible variations. Cryptic messages, they seem designed to comfort and confuse Peter and Barbara Cormin with loops of flawed recognition and to deliver them to a congenial late-evening punchiness. As the signs pop up along the highway, they take it in turn, with a rhythmic spell and counter-spell, to read the words aloud. Milk bread beer ice. Ice bread milk beer.

This marks the real death of words, thinks Barbara, these homely products reduced to husks, their true sense drained purely away. Ice beer bread milk. Rumblings in the throats, syllables strung on an old clothesline, electronic buzzing.

But, surprisingly, the short unadorned sounds, for a few minutes, with daylight fading and dying in the wide sky, take on expanded meaning. Another, lesser world is brought forward, distorted and freshly pro-visioned. She loves it–its weather and depth, its exact chambers, its lost circuits, its covered plea-sures, its submerged pattern of communication.